SALOON JUSTICE

After a row with his fiancée, young lawyer Jerry Freeman leaves New York and travels as far as his meagre savings will carry him. He ends up in the Texas town of Mineral Springs, where saloon owner Judge Clayton Singer runs a bizarre court, with the law coming second to his whims. And when Jerry, recently appointed as a public defender, takes on the wrong client, he ends up on the other side of the law himself — and in mortal peril . . .

Books by Jay Clanton
in the Linford Western Library:

QUINCY'S QUEST

JAY CLANTON

SALOON JUSTICE

Complete and Unabridged

LINFORD
Leicester

First published in Great Britain in 2014 by
Robert Hale Limited
London

First Linford Edition
published 2017
by arrangement with
Robert Hale
an imprint of The Crowood Press
Wiltshire

A catalogue record for this book is available from the British Library.

ISBN 978–1–4448–3112–2

Published by
F. A. Thorpe (Publishing)
Anstey, Leicestershire

Set by Words & Graphics Ltd.
Anstey, Leicestershire
Printed and bound in Great Britain by
T. J. International Ltd., Padstow, Cornwall

This book is printed on acid-free paper

1

I'm never going back, thought Jerry Freeman, as he picked up his bag and left the train. Not ever. The town at which he had arrived was so small that there wasn't even a proper railroad station, just a low wooden platform alongside the tracks. It was one of those places where you had to signal the driver of the train if you wanted to stop there. Still, this one horse Texas town was as far away from New York as Jerry had been able to get on the money that he had when he was buying the railroad ticket. He had changed at St Louis and now here he was in a town called, according to the sign, Mineral Springs — the best part of fifteen hundred miles from the girl he loved.

That last row had been just terrible and it was after that he had decided just to light out of town for good. It had been a cowardly and unmanly course of action to take, he knew that well enough. Still and all, there it was. There was little enough he could do about it at this late stage. Here he was, as far as his money could take him and no means at all of getting back to New York, even if he so desired.

The town itself began a hundred yards from the railroad tracks and so Jerry picked up his bag and started walking in that direction. The first building he came to, right there on the very edge of the settlement was a saloon called The Texas Rose. It was a smart enough place, with a veranda at the front. In addition to the name of the establishment, The Texas Rose, there were two more signs, one announcing that ice beer was to be had within, the other, and more prominent, giving folk to understand that Judge Clayton Singer, Notary Public, was connected to the place in some capacity. Wondering what to make of this, Jerry Freeman walked up the steps and entered The

Texas Rose in search of a long, cold drink.

The place seemed crowded, considering that it was only half past two on a Monday afternoon. Jerry would have supposed that most people would be working at this time of day, but there must have been three dozen men crammed into the bar-room. He had to wait a spell to get served and the old barkeep was disposed to be chatty. 'Stranger eh? Well you chose the right time to get here. Court Day, today. Hanging day too, if I ain't mistook.'

'Hanging? You mean somebody has been sentenced to death?'

'Not yet they ain't,' chuckled the bar tender, amused at such naivety. 'Wait till Clayton settles the business though. It's a Mexican. He hates Mexicans.'

'What's that got to do with the case?' asked Jerry curiously. The barman looked at him closely and with a certain amount of suspicion.

'From out east are you? Yes, I thought as much. You'll find we do things a bit differently round here, boy. You wait and see.'

When he had been served with his beer, which despite the advertisement outside the saloon was anything but ice cold, Jerry looked around the interior of the bar-room. It was crowded, smoky and dirty. Against one wall were two rows of chairs, one in front of the other, upon which sat twelve men. They all had glasses of liquor in their hands and half were smoking as well. What they were doing lined up like that was something of a mystery to Jerry. While he was puzzling over this, the old barkeep rapped smartly on the counter with an empty bottle and cried, 'All be upstanding for his honour, Judge Singer.'

At first, Jerry thought that this must be some kind of joke. He looked round and saw that a grimy, unshaven and dishevelled-looking middle-aged man had emerged from a door behind the bar and that everybody, including the twelve men seated by the wall, was indeed standing up. 'What the devil is this?' muttered Jerry to himself.

The grubby and unkempt fellow walked across the room to where a chair had been placed on a raised dais or platform. He took his seat there and then announced in a harsh, rasping voice, 'Court is now in session.'

Incredible as it might seem, this seedy little bar really did double as a courtroom. Jerry thought about the sign he had seen as he approached the building, with its reference to 'Judge' Clayton Singer. Why, he'd never heard of such a thing before in his life!

'Let the prisoner be brought up,' said the unappealing figure sitting on the platform. 'An' be quick about it! This here is eating into my business hours.'

In the courtrooms which Jerry had visited in New York, the command to 'Bring up the prisoner' really meant to produce him from the cells and lead him to the dock. In this court though, the instruction was obeyed literally. A trapdoor in the middle of the floor, which evidently led down to a cellar, was opened and a wretched-looking fellow hauled up. He had probably been confined in the darkness of the cellar for some little time, because he stood there blinking and screwing up his eyes, as though even the meagre amount of light to be found in this dingy room was painful to him.

'Carlos Robles,' announced the man whom Jerry now took to be Judge Singer. At the sound of his name, the man looked up hopefully. 'This court finds you charged with a grave offence agin' the dignity and peace o' the sovereign State o' Texas. To wit, a-rustlin' o' cattle. How d'you plead?'

The man who had been dragged out of the cellar seemed to understand that something was required of him, but clearly could not understand what was going on. He gabbled a few sentences in rapid and unintelligible Spanish.

Judge Singer waited until Robles had finished speaking and then, to Jerry's utter amazement, responded by saying,

'Court accepts your plea o' guilty. Jury will now deliberate and if'n it brings in any sort o' verdic' short o' hanging, it'll be held in contempt. Gentlemen, what's your verdict?'

Up to this point, Jerry Freeman had been spell-bound by the sheer, improbable grotesqueness of the scene unfolding before him. Now he marched forward and said loudly and clearly, 'What the hell is going on here?'

There was a deathly hush and Jerry was uncomfortably aware that every pair of eyes in the saloon were now turned upon him. Judge Singer was staring at him as though he had just found a cockroach in his dinner. He said, 'Young fellow, you best approach the bench and tell me what you mean by int'ruptin' the dignity of the court in this way. I'm more 'an half-minded to have you committed for contempt.'

When he was standing before Singer, the young man simply couldn't bring himself to think of the man as 'Judge', that individual said, 'Now speak out.

Tell who ye are and what you wish to say.'

'My name is Jerry Freeman and I am an Attorney at Law in New York City.'

In 1878, eleven years before Jerry Freeman fetched up in town and at a time when he was just a boy of twelve, The Texas Rose had been the only building of note among a little huddle of dwelling houses and barns which could scarcely be dignified even with the name of hamlet; let alone town. Then the railroad came, passing within a hundred yards of The Texas Rose and things began to change rapidly. At that time, Clayton Singer had not yet become a judge and was still only the owner of a saloon. The increased trade from railroad workers and passengers who visited his place for a drink while the locomotive was taking on water had the effect of making Singer the closest thing in those parts to a wealthy man.

Over the years following the arrival of the railroad, Mineral Springs began to grow. Because he owned the land between the saloon and the railroad tracks and wouldn't let anybody build there, Singer was able to ensure that this development took place in such a way that his saloon was still the first building seen by thirsty passengers. The trains seldom halted for more than ten or fifteen minutes, time only for a man to run to the saloon, gulp down a drink and then return to his seat, before he was stranded in Mineral Springs. Singer charged a dollar for a bottle of beer, which was outrageous in itself. He also made sure that if anybody handed over a five or ten dollar bill, then he was in no hurry to provide them with the change, shouting, 'In a minute, in a minute! There's others as want servin' too, you know.' When the whistle blew, signifying that the train was about to depart, those thus cheated had a straight choice; to miss their train and be stranded in Mineral Springs or to write off their money to experience. Not one man ever chose to stay in The

Texas Rose to argue out the case and so miss his train.

As the town grew, the need to maintain law and order also increased. At first, this was accomplished in an informal way by means of a vigilance committee headed by Clayton Singer. This group of citizens handed out beatings and carried out the occasional hanging. It was a rough and ready system, but ensured that the little town was never over-run with cardsharps, rustlers, thieves, rapists and other undesirable elements.

Times were changing though and in 1885 the men at the county seat decided that it was time that a Justice of the Peace was appointed to administer law in and around Mineral Springs. As head of the vigilance committee, Singer was the obvious man for the position and, after posting a thousand dollar bond, he was duly appointed Notary Public and Justice of the Peace for a vast tract of sparsely inhabited country surrounding Mineral Springs.

Clayton Singer had never found his lack of formal education any handicap in either running his saloon or maintaining law and order in the town of Mineral Springs. He didn't expect to find it a drawback in his new role as Justice of the Peace either. From somewhere, he acquired an 1848 edition of *The Revised Statutes of Texas* and studied this at odd moments between serving drinks. Singer had a good memory and within a few months he was able to quote whole chunks of the law governing the State of Texas, or at least the law which had governed it almost forty years earlier. Within a year, 'Judge' — as he had taken to calling himself — Clayton Singer could recite nigh-on the whole of that book by heart.

In a sense, Singer was a very effective Justice of the Peace, because folk took great care to keep out of his courtroom which, as Jerry Freeman discovered when he arrived in the spring of 1889, was none other than the bar-room of

The Texas Rose. In general, he was automatically prejudiced against any defendant who wasn't both white and a former member of the Confederate army. This meant that Mexicans, Chinese, blacks, Indians and northerners were apt to receive a raw deal on Mondays, when the court was sitting.

The idiosyncratic way that Clayton Singer ran his court became known to outsiders and the newspapers in Shelby County took to sending reporters to The Texas Rose on Mondays. Some of their accounts were so fantastic and amusing that papers as far afield as Boston and New York would occasionally reprint them. Singer's vocabulary and accent were always faithfully recorded. On Wednesday, September 3rd 1887, for instance, there was a fight between two men working on the new branch of the railroad, which was being constructed some five miles south of Mineral Springs. One of the men, a Chinese coolie called Ah Lok Tam, died of injuries which he received at the hands of the other participant in the brawl. The survivor ended up before Judge Singer, charged with murder. The September 18th, 1887 edition of *The Shelby County Intelligencer and Agricultural Gazette* carried the news of the trial.

Amazing Judgment in Mineral Springs Murder Trial

Regular readers of our newspaper will not be unduly surprised to learn that the most well-known luminary of the law in our own corner of the state has once again been making headlines with his highly individual way of dispensing justice in the town of Mineral Springs. Magistrate Singer, who in addition to administering justice keeps the town's saloon, had to sit in judgment on a railroad worker called Thomas Dexter. Dexter was accused of killing Ah Lok Tam, a laundry man who, claimed the defendant, had insulted him. The man was arrested and brought before Singer in his saloon, which serves on Mondays also as the local courthouse. Singer listened to the evidence, given by the accused himself, and then proceeded to turn the pages of a woefully outdated copy of the Revised Statutes. 'This here book, which is a Texas law book,' announced his honour, 'says that hommyside is th' killin' of a human, male or female. They is many kinds of hommyside — murder, manslaughter, plain hommyside, negligent hommyside, justifiable hommyside an' praise-worthy hommyside. They is three kinds o' humans — white men, negroes and Mexicans. It stan's to reason thet if a Chinym'n was human, killin' of him would come under th' head of praiseworthy hommyside. The pris'ner is discharged on condition that he pays f'r havin' th' Chinee buried.

This then was the sort of man whom the young attorney found himself standing before, after having interrupted what was apparently a capital case of stock theft.

Clayton Singer peered at the young man intently.

'Attorney, hey?' he asked, in a tone calculated to suggest that he was not overly enamoured of the breed. 'You practiced law in a courtroom?'

'Yes, sir. I mean, your honour.'

'Well, I s'pose you'll be creating if we hang this thief without due process. You want to represent him?'

'What, now?'

'Yes,' said Singer testily, 'of course now. I want my cellar back. I got other things to do with it than fill it up with Mexican bandits. You want the job? Yes or no?'

'Yes,' said Jerry slowly. 'Yes, I'll undertake his defence.'

'Well then, get on with it. We ain't got all day.'

Jerry thought for a space and then

said, 'You say that this man Robles is charged with the theft of cattle? Is the owner present here today?'

Judge Singer said, 'Jack Martin, that'd be you. Step up now and say your piece.'

A shifty and disreputable looking man shuffled to the front of the room and stood near Jerry. 'Well,' said Judge Singer, 'let's have it man. I know the story, but this boy don't.'

'Some o' my steers was stole . . . ' began Martin, but Jerry Freeman cut in at once.

'Objection. This witness has not been sworn in.'

'What then?' said the judge irritably. 'You think he'd dare tell a heap o' lies in my court? I don't think it for a moment. Carry on.'

'A man is on trial for his life,' said Jerry hotly, 'and you'd have him convicted on testimony not given on oath?'

Whatever effect the young attorney was having upon the judge, it was plain as a pikestaff that the men in the saloon were enjoying the show immensely. One or two muttered remarks such as, 'Boy's right. Let's hear him take his oath.'

The room not being too large, these observations were audible to the bench and eventually Singer gave in and called for his Bible to be fetched in from the back where it was usually kept. After Jack Martin had sworn by almighty God that the evidence he gave would be the truth, the whole truth and nothing but the truth, Jerry Freeman commenced his cross-examination.

'You say that some of your steers were stolen,' said Jerry. 'How do you know that they were stolen and did not wander off of their own accord?'

This question caused the witness to furrow his brow and think long and carefully. At length, he said, 'That greaser was found nigh to 'em . . . '

'That isn't what I asked,' said the young attorney. 'I asked how you knew that they had been stolen.'

'M' neighbour, Isaac Potter, came by

my place an' said as they'd seized a Mexican who'd taken some of my brand.'

'Do you mean to tell me that you hadn't missed the animals?'

The man shrugged, as though this was matter of little account. 'First I know of it is where Potter came by and tells me that three o' my steers had been found an' this fellow looked to be makin' off with 'em.'

'In short,' said Jerry, 'You had no reason to believe that your cattle had been stolen, other than the word of your neighbour?'

'I guess . . . '

'I'm not asking you to guess, Mr Martin. May I remind you that you are on oath? Did you have any cause to believe that your cattle had been stolen?'

'No.'

'Your honour,' said Jerry Freeman. 'I call Isaac Potter.'

It appeared that Isaac Potter was not in court and nobody had any clear notion of where he was to be found that day. At last, somebody suggested that he was involved in the well-digging a little way from the town. A couple of men volunteered to ride out and bring him to The Texas Rose. Judge Singer agreed to adjourn the case until the witness could be fetched and sworn in.

There was a great deal of lively conversation once the court was officially suspended and the bar opened again. Nobody present had ever seen the like and this trial was certainly providing more entertainment than was usual. From being an open and shut hanging matter, men were now laying bets as to the possibility of the Mexican going free.

A half hour later, Isaac Potter turned up, mightily ticked off at being dragged away from his work. The court was reconvened and Potter was sworn in. Jerry then began to question him. 'Mr Potter, you say that the defendant was taken in the act of theft?'

'Say what?' said Potter. 'The what? We talkin' 'bout that Mexican over yonder?'

'We are.'

'Well, he was waving his arms at Martin's steers, up to something, that's for certain sure.'

'What made you think that Mr Robles was stealing cattle?'

'Hard to say what else he might o' been doin' with 'em.' Isaac Potter turned to the spectators, as though expecting a round of applause or burst of laughter for his wit.

Jerry Freeman said sharply, 'May I remind you sir that a man's life is at stake. Could Mr Robles have been intercepting the steers, having seen them break out of Mr Martin's property?'

It was plain that this idea had never crossed Potter's mind. He scratched his head and then, obviously bending over backwards to appear fair, said reluctantly, 'I guess he might o' been. I just thought . . . '

'No further questions,' said Jerry hastily. He didn't want any of Potter's prejudicial speculations being aired in front of the jury. He turned to address the jury, saying, 'With his honour's permission, I would now like to remind you men that you must be satisfied beyond all reasonable doubt of this man's guilt. You alone are the judges of this case and I ask that you acquit this man now.'

All this was so novel to the twelve men sitting by the wall, that they hardly knew what to make of it. Clayton Singer normally told them what to do and since he had delegated that task, as they read the case, to this young fellow, they supposed that they should do what he told them instead. Accordingly, after some slight whispered deliberations, their spokesman stood up and said loudly, 'We find Carlos Robles not guilty.'

There was uproar in the saloon, from which Jerry Freeman took it that acquittals were by no means a common occurrence in Judge Singer's courtroom.

'All right,' said Singer irritably. 'Let the bastard go. I mean, discharge the prisoner.'

Hardly able to believe what was happening, the bewildered Mexican ran to Jerry and threw his arms around him. There were tears in the man's eyes; he had probably expected to be hanging from a nearby tree by now. It remained only for Jerry to see what the Justice of the Peace might have to say to him about his impertinence in disrupting proceedings. From what he had so far seen, Jerry rather expected to receive a string of curse words and was hugely surprised when the great man summoned him into the back room of the bar and asked, 'You lookin' for a job, young feller?'

2

While Jerry Freeman had been cross examining witnesses and addressing the jury, Clayton Singer's mind had been working fast. He had surely been vexed when that young whippersnapper had barged into his court and stirred everything up, but thinking it over, you had to admire his pluck. As the boy jabbered on, it became obvious to Singer that the men in the saloon were lapping it up. He knew that his court was a draw for those living in town and that as a consequence, The Texas Rose did better business on Mondays than on any other day of the week. He was also aware that reporters from the county newspapers came to listen as well from time to time. How though if his court became an even bigger attraction? What if visitors were drawn from far and wide to come to town and see justice done? That would surely give a boost to Mineral Springs.

So wholly unlooked for was Singer's question, that Jerry did not know what to answer. 'Well, you lookin' for a job or are ye not?' said the judge. 'It's a simple enough question and you don't suffer from any handicap in your speech, leastways from what I seen o' you so far.'

'I'm sorry sir, you just take me by surprise. What sort of job had you in mind?'

'Sloppin' out the latrines!' Singer said, displaying increasing impatience. 'Lawin' of course, what d'you think? You could defend the rascals we get here and mebbe advise on court practice and suchlike as well. What d'you say?'

The more Jerry Freeman turned the idea over in his mind, the more attractive it seemed to him. He had no money to speak of, and was effectively stranded in Mineral Springs. If he was to stay here for any length of time, then he would need work of some kind. True, advocacy work was not what he had wanted to do when he had finished law school, but he could do a lot worse right now. 'I've nowhere to live,' he said, 'But apart from that, yes, the idea suits me well enough.'

'You ain't too proud to sleep over a bar-room, I s'pose?'

'Not in the least.'

'Well, there's a room up top of here, by the roof, you can have,' said Singer. You can take your meals here too. As for money, we'll see how you go for a spell 'fore we talk o' that.'

'It's very good of you sir . . . ' began the young man. Clayton Singer cut in at once.

'None o' that nonsense, boy. I got my reasons, dare say you got yours.'

'What will I be called?' asked the young man, not that it really mattered to him.

The disreputable-looking old saloon keeper thought about this for a second or two and then said, 'What say we call you the public defender?'

After the old barkeep had shown him up to the tiny little room, which was scarcely larger than a brook closet, Jerry sat down on the bed and commenced to think things over.

The irony of the whole situation had not of course escaped him. He had fled New York in a fury as a direct consequence of this very subject; namely, whether he was to practice at the bar.

Emma, his fiancée, had been fiercely intent upon his using his legal training on behalf of ordinary people. She thought in abstract terms such as 'justice' and 'right'. It was all well and good for her to take such a principled stand; after all, her family didn't want for money. For his own part, he knew full well that the only way he would be making his fortune was in commercial work, rather than devilling in the little courts in the less salubrious boroughs of New York City. Emma's own father had made his pile through being as ruthless a businessman as anybody had ever known. His iron and steel concern had driven smaller rivals into the bankruptcy courts and secured contracts by graft and corruption of every description. And now the daughter of such a man dared to try and dictate how he, Jerry Freeman, should live his life professionally.

A month after he had finished law school, Emma had asked him plainly what his ambitions tended towards. He had told her then that his sole, immediate and direct aim was to become as wealthy as he could be. The best path for achieving that end lay in becoming a lawyer initially for one of the city's big companies and gaining experience before striking out on his own account. When he told her this, Emma had turned away, as though she did not wish to look upon his face. She said, 'Money, then, is all that you seek after your years of study?'

'I want to stand on my own two feet,' he had replied.

'What if it means stepping on other people's feet?'

'What the deuce is that supposed to mean? I only want the same as your father has. Money to live on, enough wealth to provide a home for you and me and . . . and a family.'

Emma had looked at him a little scornfully. 'The same as my father has? Is that what you want for us, Jerry? There's things which are a sight more important than money, I can tell you that. Things like honour, decency, courage and truthfulness.'

He had felt as shocked as though Emma had slapped him round the face. 'Do you say I lack those qualities?'

'No, you have them in abundance. But you won't get on in the business world without shedding them. I won't marry a man who cares only for the acquisition of money.'

Emma's idea had been that Jerry apprentice himself to some lawyer representing ordinary criminals and then work to establish a practice of his own, using his legal training for the public good. To Jerry, it sounded like madness, with the sort of future that he could have in front of him. There had been other quarrels, culminating in his breaking off the engagement, leaving New York in a fit of temper and travelling as far from the city, and Emma, as he was able.

And now here he was, stuck in this piddling little town and without the wherewithal to return to New York, at least for the time being. His grand career would have to wait a while, until he had, at the very least, earned enough to pay for a railroad ticket back to his own city. In the meantime, he was going to be following the very course of action which Emma had so forcefully urged him towards; fighting in court for the widow and orphan! He smiled ruefully at the thought.

There was a rap at the door and Jerry got up and opened it. The barkeep was standing outside. He said, 'Mr Singer says I'm to serve you two meals a day of whatever we got goin'.'

'Thank you. You're very kind.'

'Ain't kind at all. Just followin' 'structions. Clayton Singer owns this place an' who pays the piper, calls the tune. Or so they say. If'n you want to eat, we got pork and beans downstairs now. Less you're wanting room service?'

'No, no. That's fine. I'll be down directly.'

There was no sign of Judge Singer when Jerry went down to the bar-room to eat. He took the plate of food to a table by the window, hoping to be left in peace. It was not to be. No sooner had he sat down than two rough looking individuals came up and said, 'Mind if we join you, son?'

'No, please be my guest.'

The two of them stared at him disconcertingly while he ate. At last, Jerry asked, 'I take it you men were here earlier?'

'Hooee! Weren't we just,' said one of the men. 'I tell you now, we never seen the like. Thought Singer would have slain you on the spot when you stood up like that. Could o' knocked us down with a feather when he let you take over like he did.'

The other man said to his companion, 'He can be a devil when he's roused. You mind the time that fellow spent a couple o' hours drinkin' here and then swore he had no money to pay the bill?'

'Do I? That was an afternoon to recall.'

'Why,' said Jerry. 'What happened?'

'Fellow was drinking here for two hour or more. When he'd drunk his fill, he ups and tells Clayton that he's got not a cent to his name. Then he turns and walks out.'

'What happened?'

'What happened? Well may you ask. Clayton, he chases after the man and tells him as he's the judge round here. Fellow didn't give a damn, just kept on walking. Well, there was a fight and Clayton give him a black eye, knocked one o' his teeth out and hauled him back here.'

'Know what they found? Clayton searched him and he had a money belt round his waist with three hundred dollars o' gold in it. The judge, he took the money for the whiskey the man had had and then he fined him a hundred dollars, the money being to pay for — how was it he put it? — I know, 'to defray the legal expenses of pursuit, capture and return'.'

'He certainly seems a robust sort of judge,' ventured Jerry.

'Robust? You'd o' said so if you saw him the time a prisoner went for him. 'Member that Pete?'

' 'Member it? Best entertainment I seed in my whole life. T'was a fur trapper, I mind. Great big, wild lookin' creature. Looked more like a bear than man. He was bein' tried for drunkenness an' knocking some other man down. Clayton, he starts talkin' about the law of the sovereign state of Texas and this fellow, he jumps up, pulls out a bowie knife and rushed up to where the judge is sittin'. 'Law o' Texas', says he, waving this big knife in Clayton's face, 'Law o' Texas? This here is the law of Texas'.'

'What did Mr Singer do?' asked Jerry.

'Do? He weren't scared none. He whips out a six-gun and shoves it in this fellow's face and says, 'Yes, by the great Jehovah, and this here is the constitution of Texas".'

Both the men fell about laughing at the recollection of this singular incident. It was gradually dawning upon Jerry Freeman that practising law in a town like Mineral Springs would perhaps not be wholly devoid of interest.

After he had finished eating, Jerry decided to take a turn around the town and see what to make of it. There was really only one proper street, which was the one running through the centre of Mineral Springs. Other buildings were jumbled about on either side of this thoroughfare. There were the usual establishments one would expect to find in a small town; blacksmith, church, general store and so on. One of the things he soon noticed was that development of the town was being restricted because it was unable to expand towards the railroad tracks. This was, as he later learned, a consequence of Clayton Singer wishing to ensure that any passing trade from the trains which stopped to take on water, came to him and him alone in The Texas Rose. What this meant in practice was that new buildings tended to be squeezed into gaps between those which were already there; giving Mineral Springs a higgledy-piggledy appearance. The logical thing would be for new streets to be laid out towards the railroad and then for building to take place on the other side of the tracks also, so that the railroad depot was in the centre of town, rather than a hundred yards off from it. Singer though, was adamantly opposed to any such scheme and his word was, quite literally, law.

As he strolled round Mineral Springs, Jerry Freeman found that his fame had preceded him and that most of the men whom he met greeted him affably. He felt like one who has unexpectedly survived an encounter with some powerful force of nature, maybe a tornado or tidal wave. That any man would have the temerity to stand up and argue with Judge Singer in his own courtroom was an astonishing thing to the citizens of the town and Jerry was viewed as being something of a prodigy for having essayed such a rash action.

It gradually dawned upon the young attorney, as he stopped and chatted with the folk on Main Street, that Clayton Singer had somehow adopted the role of benevolent dictator in the little town. Every question he asked about the arrangement, running or future prospects of Mineral Springs was met with the replies such as, 'I don't rightly know. You'd have to ask the judge about that' or 'Mr Singer might be able to tell you' or, even when those to whom he spoke were clearly old friends of the saloon owner, 'Clayton knows about them things.'

There was no suggestion that the people who lived in the town were in fear of Singer or that he lorded it over them like some tyrant; simply that what he said went and that he was the ultimate arbiter of what should be done. This struck Jerry Freeman as being somehow unhealthy and likely to suppress development and innovation, to say nothing of discouraging competition, One of the objections which Emma had raised to his working for a big company was that many of those places, like her own father's steel mills, were monopolies in all but name. She had advanced the thesis that such a state of affairs was unhealthy and worked to oppose progress and freedom. He hadn't quite seen what she was driving at when they were discussing the question in the comfortable surroundings of the parlour of a big house in New York, but he thought now that he could see what she meant. This town was fit to grow and expand, become a bustling new place which would thrive in all kinds of different ways, but Clayton Singer wanted it to remain just the same as it had always been, with his the only saloon in town and his word law on everything from new buildings to what hours the store could open. It was the old way, a bit like medieval times from what Jerry recalled reading of them at school, with one leader telling all the other folk for miles around how to live their lives. What they used to call 'The Feudal System'. Those ways were gone now though, only lingering on in a handful of out-of-the-way locations like this.

While he was musing along these lines, Jerry almost bumped into a young woman coming out of the store. She was a pert-looking creature and when Jerry nearly knocked the basket from her hands, she said, 'Mind where you're walking now.'

'Sorry ma'am, the fault was entirely my own.'

'My,' said the girl, looking at him closely, 'but don't you speak nice? New boy in town, I should say.'

'That's about the strength of it, ma'am.'

'Less of the ma'am,' she said tartly. 'It makes me sound like somebody's aunt. My name's Maria Fallon. You can call me Miss Fallon or Maria if you prefer. I don't much mind which.'

It would have felt awfully familiar to start addressing a young woman by her Christian name within a minute of meeting her and so he said, 'I'm very pleased to meet you, Miss Fallon.'

The girl, who could not have been much over eighteen years of age, wrinkled her nose, saying, 'Well, it's an improvement, but it still makes me seem like an old maid. I'll warrant you're the fellow who stopped the hanging this afternoon?'

'I am.'

'Well done,' she said emphatically. 'It's plain disgraceful how that man deals out death like he was a Roman emperor or some such.'

'I got the feeling that most folk round here are happy enough with the way things are run,' said Jerry diffidently. 'You're the first to say that there's something wrong.'

The girl looked at him, as though trying to gauge how much she could say to this complete stranger. In the end, she said, 'People like what they're familiar with. They don't welcome change. And having a strong man in charge means not having to think too much for themselves.' Then, worried perhaps that she had said too much, she continued, 'Well, I best get back with these provisions or there'll be no meal tonight for my family.'

'Your family?' exclaimed Jerry, before he could stop himself. 'You mean you're married?' Then he recollected himself and stopped, feeling his cheeks redden. How could he have spoken so to an unknown woman?

Maria Fallon burst into a peal of girlish laughter, which caused an old woman passing by to remark to her companion that young girls these days were mighty fast to tip their hats at any passing stranger. 'Lord,' she said, 'Do I look that old? No, I'm taking this home for my step-mother to prepare. But I can't stand chatting to you all day, I'll scandalize folks. Goodbye, it was good to meet you.'

Jerry Freeman stood staring after the girl as she made her way down Main Street and it was in this uncouth attitude that his first paying client discovered him. There was a discreet cough behind him and when he looked round, Jerry found that a man who had 'farmer' written all over him was standing at his elbow. 'May I help you, sir?' he enquired politely.

'You really a lawyer?'

'That I am. Qualified this year.'

'Know aught about wills and such, do you?'

'Why yes, I'm pretty familiar with the law of probate. Why do you ask?'

'My name's Coolidge and I got a will to make. I'm ill, like as not dying, and want to get my affairs in order. I'll pay.'

'When would you like me to call, sir? I'm afraid I have no office.'

'Don't want you to call. I wants you to come with me now. You got paper and pen? I surely have none such in my house.'

'I have some in my bag, but we'll have to go by the saloon to fetch it.'

The man who wanted to make out his will didn't, to Jerry's eyes, look particularly sick. Still and all, he wasn't a medical doctor and was really no sort of judge of those things. When they got to Mr Coolidge's house, he proved to be living alone; having, at least according to his own account, fallen out with every living member of his family.

Once they got to the farmer's house, which was the better part of a forty-five minute walk from town, it didn't take above half an hour to complete the man's will, which essentially left all he possessed to an old drinking companion. 'Not that I like the fellow over-much,' confided Coolidge, 'but I'll be damned if I let my family get a sniff of me money.' After they went to a neighbour to find two people to witness the will, Coolidge asked how much he owed. This put Jerry Freeman into something of a quandary, because he was too embarrassed to tell this man that he was the very first client of Jerry's professional life. The farmer noticed his hesitation and said, 'You done this before? No? Thought as much. Anybody can see that you're full young to be a lawyer. What would you say to five dollars?'

'I'd say thank you very much, Mr Coolidge,' said Jerry, grateful to the man for easing him out of an embarrassing dilemma.

3

Over the course of the next week or so, Jerry Freeman began to get a feel for the way that Mineral Springs was run and the more he saw, the more he realized what an anachronism the little town was.

To begin with, there was no official law enforcement. Clayton Singer might be an officially appointed Justice of the Peace, sanctioned from the county seat, but his real authority lay in his having been the leader of the vigilance committee which until a few years ago ran things in the town. There was no sheriff or marshal within fifty miles of Mineral Springs, which meant that if any criminal needed to be captured, it was done in an informal way by several men banding together into a posse. In fact, the administration of law and order in the town had not really changed over the last fifty years or so. Singer's trials were all but indistinguishable from the kind of kangaroo court one might have seen forty years earlier during the California Gold Rush.

Towns like Mineral Springs though were slowly being forced to change. The tentacles of civilization were spreading out from the east and north of the nation, until they would eventually bring a regulated legal system to every nook and cranny of the United States. Although he didn't realize it at the time, Jerry Freeman himself was a harbinger of this change. There had never been a genuine lawyer in the town, a man who knew what the legal position was in the better regulated parts of the country. Although appointing him to a semi-official position, attached to his 'court', had been a whim of Singer's, it also marked the beginning of a change in attitude of the men and women in the town. Although a lot of those who lived in Mineral Springs were semi-literate and ignorant of many of the finer points of civil society which might be taken for granted in and around Washington, they had a respect for learning and recognized in the young attorney a representative from a different and more sophisticated world than that which they knew.

Before Jerry's arrival, those with a dispute over land or property would bring their grievances before Clayton Singer on Monday afternoons at The Texas Rose. The problem was that everyone knew of the Justice of the Peace's partiality and deep-rooted prejudices. It was also widely known that he was a corrupt and venial man; one who was not at all averse to being slipped a bribe before he pronounced judgment in civil cases. Worst of all, despite his impressive ability to parrot great chunks from the Revised Statutes, Singer had no real understanding of law and the legal system.

It was immensely flattering for a young fellow of just twenty-three years of age to find himself being consulted and listened to respectfully by men old enough to be his grandfather. In New York, a newly qualified attorney of Jerry Freeman's age would have been a very small tiddler in an exceedingly large pond. Here, he was treated as a combination of Coke, Blackstone and Solomon!

Many of those wanting advice, pumped Jerry in a way that they evidently thought right cunning, asking him hypothetical questions along the lines of, 'My friend has a difficult problem'. This of course enabled them to consult a qualified lawyer for nothing. He didn't mind this, because like so many young folk, he was glad of the chance to show off a little. The week wore away in this fashion, until Sunday came round and Jerry found himself looking forward with interest to appearing once more in Judge Singer's court. Before that though, there was a sensational incident.

Fortunately for Jerry Freeman, he

was walking in the hills around Mineral Springs and so was not a witness to the events which led to the trial for murder the following day of Xaviera Ramirez. Had he seen what happened, then he would have thought himself duty-bound not to take part in the subsequent trial in any capacity, bar that of witness. In fact, after attending church in the morning, Jerry had offered to walk Maria Fallon home; a proposal which that young lady accepted with alacrity. Like most everybody else in town, she was intrigued by the good-looking young lawyer and wanted to know what made him tick.

In England and on the east coast of America, the 'New Woman' was just beginning to be talked about, but Maria knew nothing of such developments. She was only aware that the traditional role of women was not too inviting and she was sick and tired of the countless restrictions which were placed upon her life and conduct. This manifested itself in her being a little more forward in the way that she spoke and behaved than was acceptable in a small Texas town. Some of the older and more conservative women had already privately passed judgment on the girl and their verdict was that she was 'bold' and 'fast'.

As they walked towards the farm where she lived with her father and stepmother, Maria said suddenly, 'You know, they say that you have fetched up here because there's a woman in the case. That you've been crossed in love or some such.'

To his chagrin, Jerry felt himself blushing like a schoolgirl. The girl walking at his side shot him a sidelong glance and then said saucily, 'Ah, you needn't say any more on the subject, Mr Freeman. I see that there's something in it.'

'It's not a matter of saying anything more,' he replied irritably. 'I've said nothing at all so far, so I can hardly say anything more.'

'You mean you couldn't have said anything less,' said Maria and then immediately regretted her pertness, because she saw that the young man was genuinely put out. She reached out her hand and touched his arm, saying, 'Don't you mind me. I always talk too much.'

There was an uncomfortable silence until they reached the edge of the fields owned by the Fallon family, when Jerry found the tables neatly turned. Anybody wondering where Maria Fallon got her outspokenness from, or her impatience with what she saw as petty restrictions and foolish conventions, would only have to spend five minutes or so in the company of her father Albert. It was he who had taught his daughter to be an independent creature and he who encouraged her to seek a little more from life than that of the average farmer's daughter in that part of Texas.

Albert Fallon was hoeing a field by the side of the track which led to his house. He was a hale and broad-shouldered man in his mid-forties. Notwithstanding his age, he could outpace many a twenty year-old when it came to working or drinking. When he saw the young couple approaching, he stood up and walked over to them. Putting on a forbidding look, he said gruffly to Jerry, 'Now then, young man. Are you a-courting of my daughter? Should I be asking you your intentions?'

At this, Maria flushed deep crimson and struck her father hard upon the arm. 'Hush now, Pa,' she said. 'What will Mr Freeman think of us?'

'Meaning, what will he think of you,' said her father shrewdly. The blush did not leave her cheeks and she saw that Jerry Freeman had observed it, which threw her into even greater confusion.

'Only kidding, Mr Freeman,' said Fallon amiably. 'There's not all that much in the way of amusement in this district and so we are forced to provide our own. No offence meant.'

'None taken, sir.'

'Would you be wanting to come to dinner, later in the week?' asked Albert Fallon. 'I'm tolerable familiar with most of those as lives round here and a new face might make a pleasant change. Eh, Maria?'

But the girl was seriously annoyed with her father and made no reply. Jerry said, 'That's very good of you, sir. What day had you in mind?'

'What about Thursday?'

Just as Jerry was about to assent to the arrangement, there came from far away the sound of a volley of gunfire. 'Hallo,' said Fallon. 'What's to do? That came from town, or I miss my guess.'

Ramirez had tracked his one-time partner for over three hundred miles now. He had followed him across the border into the United States and pursued him remorselessly, with the single-minded determination of a wolf or other beast of prey. Had it just been the money which Cordero had taken, then perhaps Ramirez would have given up after the man who had betrayed him crossed the Rio Grande. But that had not been all that had been stolen from him. When word had come that Cordero was gone, Xaviera Ramirez had seen something unmistakable in his own wife's face.

It had taken over an hour for Ramirez to beat the truth from his wife and when he had done so, he felt as though his whole life was ruined. His best friend had betrayed him, stolen his fortune and also destroyed his marriage. But he had left him one precious gift, something which nobody could snatch away from Ramirez: the chance of revenge.

For almost a month, Ramirez had trailed his one-time friend across Texas. At times, the trail had gone cold and he was obliged to double back and search for signs of the man. Cordero had an instinct which must have told him that he was being followed, because he rode like the wind, weaving back and forth, never keeping a straight course. But everything comes to an end eventually, and Ramirez came across his quarry in the first light of dawn. The first that Hector Cordero knew of his impending death was a sharp, metallic click in his ear, as Ramirez cocked his pistol.

At first, Cordero had it in mind to go for his weapon, but then he saw that his old friend had taken the precaution of removing all his clothes and even his boots, in which Cordero habitually secreted a little muff pistol. The devil of riding with a man for so long is that he is apt to learn all little secrets of this kind.

'So Hector,' Ramirez had said, 'are you ready to die?'

'All things are with God,' said the other, piously. 'If I die today, then tomorrow it will be your turn.'

'Get up and remove the rest of your clothes.'

There seemed to Hector Cordero little choice but to obey. When the fear of death is upon you, even the few extra seconds that it takes to remove your socks is a welcome respite. 'What, then?' Cordero asked, once he was standing there completely naked.

'Now, you run. I will give you ten minutes' start. Then I will come after you and kill you slowly. I will come on foot, I would not wish to finish the game too quickly.'

'But . . . ' said Cordero.

'The clock is running, old friend,' said Ramirez implacably.

Incredibly, it took the hunter over five hours to run down his prey. The idea of the frightened, naked man running in terror from him had appealed to Ramirez and it had not occurred to him that his would be anything other than a few minutes' sport: a cat playing with a helpless mouse. But Cordero had run into the little wood which lay alongside his camping place and, skilled as he was in reading the tracks of men, Ramirez was foxed now. A man's boots leave a far clearer trail than that of the bare foot and Cordero, it must be remembered, was playing for his very life.

It was almost midday before the game came to an end, when Ramirez arrived at the crest of a hill and saw his old friend stumbling towards a little town. The hunter quickened his pace and practically ran down the hill, reaching the main street of Mineral Springs at the same time as his adversary.

Cordero was in a pitiful state, with his feet bloodied and torn. He was panting from exhaustion and, to Ramirez's eye, he had the look of a hunted animal on the verge of collapse. This was just precisely what Ramirez had been hoping for. When he caught sight of the man who had been pursuing him so remorselessly, Hector Cordero shrieked aloud in English, 'For the love of God, help me! Murder!'

It being Sunday, there were not as many people in and around Main Street as usual, but his cries brought a few people out to see what all the shouting was about. 'Mother of God, have mercy upon me!' shouted Cordero frantically.

The wife of the man who ran the general store had come out of the living quarters at the back of the store and she went over to the desperate man, buck naked though he was. Then she saw the man standing in the shadows, perhaps twenty yards away. She said, 'What's going on? What are you threatening this poor fellow for?'

Hardly were the words out of her mouth, when Ramirez raised his rifle and fired once at Cordero, hitting him in the belly. Blood splashed onto Mrs Cartwright and she watched, paralysed with fear as Ramirez drew his pistol and fired again at the naked man beside her. This shot took him in the thigh. Her husband had come out and was yelling at her to get away out of it, but she could by no means reconcile such a course of action with her Christian duty and attempted to shield Cordero from further harm, by moving in front of him and blocking him from the view of the gunman.

It was at this point that Ramirez made the move which sealed his death warrant. Even at this point, with a bloody murder actually being committed on the streets of the town, it was possible that the citizens of Mineral Springs might have overlooked the affair and regarded it as a private quarrel between two excitable foreigners. After all, if one Mexican wanted to shoot another, it was no great matter to most of those living thereabouts. All that went by the board when Ramirez walked forward and then raised his gun and again fired at the wounded man. This time, the bullet hit Cordero in the chest, killing him on the spot. Before it entered the man's heart though, this bullet sliced through the arm of the good woman who was doing her best to protect the helpless victim from his attacker. It wasn't a serious wound, more like a deep graze than anything else, but it was more than enough to excite the indignation and wrath of those who were now gathering in Main Street, attracted by the novel sound of gunfire.

Before Xaviera Ramirez could get off another shot, he was jumped from behind, knocked to the ground and disarmed. When it was seen that the popular Mrs Cartwright, one of the kindest and most inoffensive women in the town, had been wounded, the men around Ramirez began knocking him about.

Now ten years before this incident, it is highly likely that the Mexican would have been hoisted from the nearest tree and the entire business would have been over and done with in a matter of minutes. Times had changed though. At the very least, when they had finished kicking and punching Ramirez, the men who had caught him felt that it would be necessary to take him to Clayton Singer to see what he wanted to do. Jerry Freeman would perhaps have been surprised to know that his presence in town too had a moderating effect on the behaviour of the men. Knowing that they had in their town a genuine, honest-to-God New York attorney made everybody slightly more careful about legal niceties than they might otherwise have been. It was almost like they were in some way being on their best behaviour.

It wasn't needful to drag Ramirez all the way to the saloon, because Judge Singer himself appeared on the scene. He too had been drawn there upon hearing the shots. When he realized that Mrs Cartwright had been injured by the damned Mexican laying in the dust, Singer had an almost irresistible urge to order the fellow's summary execution. Strange to relate, he too paused, wondering what the boy from New York would make of such a proceeding. He settled for lashing out savagely with his boot at the man's head. 'Hogtie him and bring him along with me,' he said. 'He'll hang all right, but let's do the thing properly.'

It was while the Mexican was being bound hand and foot that Jerry Freeman turned up, having sprinted all the way from the edge of the Fallon farm. 'What's happening?' he asked.

'Happenin'?' said Singer. 'I tell you what's happenin'. Yon savage has killed a man and hurt one o' the best women as ever took breath.'

'What are you going to do with that man? He looks hurt as well.' There were some grounds for saying this, as Ramirez had been kicked almost senseless by the men who had surrounded him after he was disarmed. Jerry noticed to his disgust that there were three gleaming white teeth laying in the road, each nestling in a shining pool of spittle and blood. Ramirez's face was also bloodied, from where a blow had connected with his nose.

'Hurt, is he?' asked Singer. 'Well now, we ain't got no hospital in this town, so I reckon as he'll have to make do with the next best thing.'

'Where's that?' asked Jerry innocently.

'My cellar,' said Singer.

The shooting in town was the greatest sensation for some good, long while. Taking place on a Sunday, as it did, meant that many folk did not feel properly able to gossip about it until the next day. It was, after all, the Lord's day and it would not have felt right to discuss a murder in salacious detail on the one day of the week when one's thoughts were supposed to be turned to higher matters. Behind doors and window shades, the matter was discussed at length, but the convention was respected after church that evening that only general expressions of horror at the depravity which surrounded them were to be allowed. People remarked, one to the other, as they walked home, 'Ah, there's a deal of wickedness in the world.'

While he was eating that evening, Judge Singer came over to Jerry's table and sat himself down without asking leave. Being a Sunday, the saloon was closed and so they were able to talk privately. As soon as he sat down, Singer said, 'You'll be wantin' to go through the motions tomorrow, I s'pose?'

'I'm sorry,' said the young attorney, 'I don't rightly understand you.'

'That damned rascal as shot Cartwright's wife. Him as is down beneath our feet as we talk.'

'Well,' said Jerry, 'I don't know what you mean by, 'going through the motions'. If you mean will I be defending him, then yes, of course. That's what you hired me for, isn't it?'

'For sure. Just don't waste too much time on it, that's all. We got other stuff to get through tomorrow.'

'Tomorrow? You're not planning to bring this man to trial twenty four hours after the arrest, surely?'

Singer looked puzzled at Jerry Freeman's tone. 'No sense in hangin' around, I'd o' thought. Sooner we get it over with the better. Better for that bastard too, I should say.'

'Mr Singer, Judge I mean, you can't be serious? I'll need time to speak to my client and take his instructions. I know nothing about the affair.'

'You got 'til tomorrow afternoon,' said Singer inexorably. 'And like I say, don't bother too hard, 'cause it won't make a mort o' difference. I aim to see that man hanging before the sun goes down.'

4

Sunday night saw Jerry Freeman burning the midnight oil, quite literally. Until well past two on Monday morning, he was sitting in his room at the top of the saloon, trying desperately to work out some sort of a defence. He knew the bare facts of the case and they did not look at all promising for his client. Unless he was able to come up with some unexpected circumstance as a result of the interview with the prisoner which Singer had promised him, then it was like the Bible said: making bricks without straw. He had nothing at all to work with.

When he left New York, Jerry had taken with him one or two of his law books; Mayhew's Court Practice and Robinson on Tort, for instance. Nothing in any of those books seemed to offer the slightest mitigation for a case of murder such as had been described to him. From all that he was able to apprehend, a naked man had staggered into town and almost immediately afterwards been shot down by the man now locked in the cellar. What mitigation or defence could there be, given the circumstances? At half past two, Jerry turned down the wick and extinguished the lamp and then slept soundly through for the next seven hours.

The Texas Rose was due to open at midday and with the prospect of a murder trial, Clayton Singer expected to do roaring business. He rather grudgingly hauled the prisoner up from the cellar for half an hour before opening and then sat across the room, with his pistol drawn, glowering at Ramirez. Jerry had been very firm in his insistence that the judge should not be within earshot of the consultation, to which Singer had reluctantly assented.

'I'm sorry,' said Jerry to the man, whose hands were still bound and who presented a pitiful spectacle, 'I don't even know your name or whether you speak English.

'I speak English and my name is Ramirez, Xaviera Ramirez.'

'Would you like to tell me what happened yesterday, Mr Ramirez?'

'You have not heard? I shot that bastard-pig down in the dirt. I am not sorry. Why should I be?'

'Well for one thing, unless I'm very much mistaken, folk round here have it in mind to hang you today. Doesn't that make you sorry?'

The man in front of him shrugged. 'All men die one day. You pay for your pleasures in this world. I shot Cordera and now I must pay for it. That is how the life works.'

'Cordera? Was that the dead man's name?'

Ramirez shrugged indifferently. 'Does it matter what his name was called?'

'Why did you shoot him?' asked Jerry and, after looking for a space into the eyes of the eager young man who seemed so keen to save his life, the Mexican sighed and began to tell the story of his sorrow.

There were normally a few more people in town for Court Day; generally, those who lived on farms near Mineral Springs. But this Monday surpassed all Clayton Singer's expectations. He didn't think that all the new faces could have been drawn here just by the murder yesterday. It was hardly possible that news about this could have spread so rapidly. No, it was as he had suspected. For the last week, everybody had been talking about the bold young Easterner who had jumped up in his court and challenged him about the fate of that wretched rustler. They'd all come to watch Jerry Freeman in action. Well, the fact that they would be witnessing a murder trial and execution would surely mean that word would spread even farther and that next week, there would be even greater crowds. Singer congratulated himself on his shrewdness. He just knew that it was a smart move to install that young lawyer in this place. He was worth ten times as much as he was costing in the two meagre meals each day which he was eating at The Texas Rose.

After he had bundled Ramirez back into his cellar and bolted the trapdoor, Singer took a turn around the town to get a feel for how the mood was running. One of the things that had made him such a successful leading figure in Mineral Springs was that he always managed to gauge the mood of people pretty accurately and tailored his actions accordingly. This morning, after getting the barkeep to open up, Singer strolled along Main Street, listening with half an ear to what was being said. There could be no doubt that the mood was running very high against the Mexican whose trial was to take place that very day. Some in the town were of the opinion that in such a clear cut and obvious case, then it was weak-minded shilly-shallying to hold any sort of trial and that the man should have been strung up on the spot. Mingled with this extreme sentiment however, was the majority view that it was very right and proper that the killer should be subject to due legal process, as long as this didn't prevent him from being hanged that afternoon.

As for the so-called Public Defender, he was eagerly awaiting the chance to spring a mine on the court, for he had come up with what he thought might just possibly be a defence against the charge of murder which Xaviera Ramirez was facing.

Promptly at half past two that afternoon, the barkeep rapped on the counter and required all present to be upstanding for his honour, Judge Clayton Singer. When the judge had taken his place on the raised dais, he called the court to order and requested all persons having any business to draw near. He then called for the prisoner to be brought up, which, having been done, Singer gave those present to understand that the man was charged with murder and malicious wounding. Before the trial commenced, Jerry Freeman stood up and asked if he might speak. Singer granted his request with an exceedingly ill grace. 'Yes, Mr Freeman, you go right ahead,' before adding, sotto voce, 'and little enough good it will do you and your client.'

'Your honour, may it please the court, my client pleads not guilty and enters a special defence of temporary insanity.'

There was a subdued murmur at this; folk wondering what the Sam Hill the young lawyer was up to.

'You say tempo'ry insanity?' asked Judge Singer, making no effort to conceal his scorn.

'Yes, it is my contention that this is a *crime passionale*.'

'A cream *what?*' said Singer. 'Sounds like somethin' you'd have in a fancy restaurant.' This produced a ripple of sycophantic laughter.

'A crime of passion,' said Jerry

Freeman. 'If you'd prefer it in plain English.'

'Yeah, let's try and keep it in English, hey?'

Witnesses were called who recounted the scene on Main Street when Ramirez killed the man he had been pursuing. Mrs Cartwright, her arm tied up in a sling, was also ushered in and gave her account of the incident. Being such a godly and upright woman, she had never in her life been in the saloon before and looked round with undisguised curiosity; like one of the righteous who finds himself on a day-excursion to Sodom or Gommorah.

After it had been established to general satisfaction that the prisoner had shot both the man he killed and also Mrs Cartwright, the Public Defender was invited to outline the case for the defence. Jerry stood up, opened a book which he had in his hand and said, 'I wish to cite the case of District of Columbia versus Daniel Sickles, 1859.'

'Go on then, son,' said Judge Singer, raising his eyes to the heavens and shaking his head wearily, catching the eyes of the jury as he did so.

'As your honour will no doubt recall,' began Jerry tactfully, 'this case concerned Congressman Daniel Sickles. On February 26th 1859, he discovered that his wife was having an adulterous affair with Philip Barton Key, who happened, to the discredit of my chosen profession, to be an attorney.' There were a few chuckles at this, which caused Judge Singer to growl.

'I'll make the jokes, Mr Freeman.'

'The following day, after having slept on the matter, the Congressman saw Key hanging around outside his house, whereupon he rushed out and emptied a pistol at the man, who was killed. At his trial, he was acquitted, having been adjudged to be temporarily insane.'

There was dead silence in the saloon. Every man there could well imagine doing the same thing, given similar circumstances and indeed, some knew of such cases; none of which had ever progressed as far as getting anywhere near a courtroom.

'Well?' said Singer. 'What's your point?'

'Only this. Xaviera Ramirez, the unhappy man you see before you, was himself betrayed by his best friend. He pursued him in a fit of madness and when he found him, fell upon him and shot him, just like Congressman Daniel Sickles. Gentlemen of the jury, we do not have one law in this country for Congressmen and another for penniless wanderers. All are alike under the law. I call upon you to acquit Mr Ramirez.'

Nobody, not even Judge Singer, said anything for a few seconds after this speech. Then the judge felt that it was time to point out one or two things. He asked Jerry, 'How long ago did this fit o' madness come on this man? How long's he been a chasin' of this other feller?'

Jerry Freeman had been hoping against hope that nobody would ask this question, but he didn't want to tell a direct lie, even in such a courtroom as this. He said, 'I believe for a period of a month or so.'

'A month!' exclaimed Singer in astonishment. 'You're tryin' to put it across us that this damned . . . that the defendant has been insane for a month?'

There was no reply and Judge Singer followed up his advantage by saying, 'What about the poor woman as he shot? Was that part o' his madness as well?'

'Mr Ramirez is deeply sensible of the pain he has caused Mrs Cartwright and wishes to apologize to the court for the suffering he inadvertently inflicted upon an innocent person.'

'Yes,' said Singer, 'I'll take oath he does, now as he stands in the shadow of the rope. I heard enough o' this. You men in the jury, it's up to you to decide. You got any questions?'

The twelve grim-faced men sitting in a double row against the wall did not have any questions and nor did they wish to deliberate. They had their verdict ready and waiting and that verdict was 'Guilty'.

'May I make a speech in mitigation?' asked Jerry, hoping against hope that he would still be able to do something for the man.

'No point,' said Singer brusquely. 'It's capital murder. I sentence the accused to hang by the neck. He can have a drink afore he goes. What you havin' feller?'

'Whiskey, if you please,' said Ramirez politely. 'You might make it a large one.'

Even Judge Singer could not help admiring such coolness. He said to the barkeep, 'Give him a large whiskey. Untie his hands and feet.'

Jerry Freeman went up to the judge and said, 'What's the procedure now, Judge?'

Singer seemed surprised at the question. He said, 'Procedure? Why, we take him out o' town a-ways and hang him.'

Jerry Freeman had spent his whole life in and around New York. He had always been vaguely aware that capital punishment was inflicted upon murderers, but fortunately, the whole business took place behind closed doors in prisons. That being so, he had never really given the subject any sustained thought. It was, he supposed, a distasteful necessity and he was heartily glad that he was not called upon himself either to witness or participate in the grisly ritual.

Ramirez sipped his drink, looking as though he was savouring every slight nuance of the taste and smell of it — as well he might, he would be unlikely to have another glass of whiskey in the near future. When he had finished it, he set the glass down delicately upon the counter and said, 'I am ready.'

In Mineral Springs, the occasional hangings were viewed as being a part of the natural order. When the procession left The Texas Rose, any men, women and even children in the street nearby, drifted along to see what would happen. It was, to Jerry Freeman's more sophisticated, city perspective, perfectly ghastly. At his side, a boy who could be no older than eleven walked along, obviously intending to witness the execution.

Jerry had always imagined that a man being led to his own death would be in a state of collapse, perhaps needing to be dragged along like an ox to the slaughter. In fact Ramirez sauntered towards the tall oak tree as though he were taking a morning constitutional before breakfast. Something which the young attorney marked and which made a great impression upon him when thinking over the scene later, was when the condemned man came to a pile of horse manure. He walked around it fastidiously, anxious not to get it on his boots. This little human detail made the whole business seem more terrible. Here was a man who, like the rest of us, didn't wish to get muck on his boots and yet within a matter of minutes, he would be dead.

When the crowd reached the tree, there was a slight delay, while they waited for the man who was charged with bringing the horse and rope. Once he arrived, things happened very swiftly. A noose was made in the rope and it was flung over a branch, then lowered until it dangled seven or eight feet from the ground. While this was being done, somebody else tied the Mexican's hands behind his back. He was then manhandled on to the back of the horse and the beast led to where the noose was waiting.

Ramirez allowed these things to be done to him without offering any resistance. Later, as he tossed and turned in his bed that night, Jerry came to the conclusion that the fellow probably wanted to get the whole thing over with as quickly as possible. Fitting the noose around the mounted man's neck was a tricky business, it being done by men on the ground who had to reach high up, but Ramirez obligingly bent down his neck, so that the thing could the more easily be accomplished. He acted for all the world as though he were at the barber's shop.

Once the noose was secured, another man wound the rope round and round a low branch, being careful to maintain tension on the rope while he was doing so. Then he tied a knot to hold it in place. That was something else that struck the young lawyer; this execution was very much a joint effort, with many citizens taking an active role. It put him in mind of a stoning to death out of the Old Testament.

Judge Singer stepped forward and said, 'Well, you been properly convicted. Even had a lawyer to defend you.'

Ramirez said, 'I make no complaint.'

'Well, you had your fun, now it's time to pay. Got anything to say, 'fore we carry out the sentence?'

Ramirez looked around at the crowd of men and women. For the first time, he looked a little sad and regretful. His eyes lit upon Jerry Freeman and he said, 'I have nothing to say, except to thank that young fellow who tried to help me. I wish him well.'

'That it?' asked Singer.

Ramirez nodded and licked his lips. Then Singer stepped forward and slapped the horse on the rump. The mare whinnied and jittered, but did not move and so the judge gave her a harder slap, upon which she bolted forward, leaving the Mexican dangling in the air.

Horrified though he was, Jerry could not take his eyes from the hideous sight of a fellow being choked to death at the end of a rope. Ramirez died hard; kicking and struggling for fully five minutes. After it was over, some of the men, who had seen a number of hangings, gave it as their opinion that the condemned man had had powerful neck muscles, which meant that death from strangulation would be slower in coming.

As he was leaving the hanging, Jerry

saw to his disgust that Maria Fallon was standing and watching. He seized her arm roughly and hustled her to one side. 'What the devil are you doing here?' he asked.

'You ain't my pa,' said the girl, struggling to free her arm from his grip. 'It's no affair of yours where I am.'

'How could you watch such a thing?'

'I didn't notice you closing your eyes,' she said sharply, 'or will you tell me that you were here out of duty?'

Jerry let go of her arm, stung by her words. It was on the tip of his tongue to tell her that he had attended the execution because he was an officer of the court. As he took breath to do so, he knew that it would be a lie. He could, had he been minded, have hung back or simply gone to his room. Nobody would have noticed or even cared had he done so. Truth was, he had come to see the hanging out of morbid curiosity, purely and simply because he had never seen a man done to death before.

'Yes,' said Maria Fallon. 'That gave you pause, I'll warrant. You came for the self-same reason as everybody else. Because the sight of a man being killed is thrilling and folk like to gloat over the fact that they're still alive and some poor soul is not. It's the most ghoulish thing I ever heard tell of.'

'It's done on our behalf. We shouldn't be afraid to see it done. That's the first time ever I saw such a thing. It would have been cowardly to hide away from it.'

'It's the first hanging I ever seen, too,' said Maria. 'It was the worst thing I saw in my life.'

Without saying anything, the two of them turned and began to stroll back towards The Texas Rose. It was remarked by some of those who had lately watched the execution that the Fallon girl surely was throwing herself at that young lawyer. Maybe somebody should speak to her father; it was downright indecent, the show she was making of herself.

'You're still coming to dinner on Thursday night, I suppose?' asked Maria.

'If the invitation stands, I am.'

'Well then be sure to come at about seven.'

The girl turned and walked away from Jerry without another word, leaving him feeling rather dissatisfied about his own conduct and wondering if he could have presented himself to better advantage.

Jerry Freeman didn't see Singer again, until later that evening. He went for a long walk, wanting to be by himself. When the judge bumped into him as he was going up to his room, he said to Jerry, 'You did your best for that worthless piece of trash. He was guilty as Cain and we both know it.'

Jerry was honest enough to say, 'Yes, I think you're right.'

'He would o' been hanged just the same in New York, I'll wager. Just would have taken 'em longer and they'd o' made more of a production of it, that's all.'

This was pretty well what the lawyer had already concluded and so there was little that he could say, other than, 'Goodnight, sir.'

In the course of Tuesday and Wednesday, Jerry was engaged for just two pieces of legal work. One was drawing up a lease for a man who wished to rent out a building and the other was another will. He received twelve dollars in fees for these trifling pieces of work. At this rate, thought Jerry Freeman to himself, it is going to take me a good long while before I even make enough to pay for a ticket back to New York, never mind return there having made my fortune.

Thoughts of Maria Fallon were also occupying the attorney's mind and he found himself looking forward to going to visit her and her family on Thursday. It's not as though he was in love with her, he thought to himself, but she struck him as being entertaining company. In truth, he missed Emma dreadfully as the days passed. He wondered what she would think if she could see him now, spending his days grubbing out a living as a small town lawyer; doing in fact, just precisely what she had wanted him to do. How ridiculous that he should have fled fifteen hundred miles like this, only to end up doing the very thing that he had wished to avoid. Jerry supposed that there must be a moral there somewhere if only you cared to look hard enough.

Mrs Cartwright's arm was healing well enough and she seemed none the worse for being shot. It was touching to see that she had made the arrangements for the funeral of both the Mexican who had been shot in front of her and also his killer. It seemed to Jerry that here was an example of true Christian charity in practice; a rare enough thing to come across.

The days passed pleasantly enough until Thursday dawned. While eating breakfast, Jerry wondered if he ought to take some little gift to Maria's family as a token of his appreciation for being asked to a meal there. He knew that in New York, a bunch of flowers or a box of candy would be considered acceptable and decided to follow the same line here. That morning, he made his way to the general store and found Mrs Cartwright behind the counter. She seemed pleased to see him.

'Why, it's Mr Freeman, isn't it? What can we do for you, young man?'

'I'm going to dinner tonight, I thought I'd take some candy or something as a gift.' Mrs Cartwright looked at him a little oddly and he said, 'That's the sort of thing I'd do back home. If I'd been invited to somebody's house for a meal, that is.'

'Listen here, I'm old enough to be your grand mama. You won't mind me giving you a piece of advice, maybe?'

'No,' said Jerry gratefully. 'I'd be glad if you would. I don't rightly know what's considered fitting in here.'

'Are you aiming to show some girl that you're sweet on her?' she asked bluntly.

'Lord, no,' said Jerry, horrified at the construction that was being put upon his innocent gift. 'Not a bit of it. Why?'

'In these parts, a young man like you fetching up at a house containing a young lady while carrying a box of candy is next door to a proposal of marriage. At the least, it says you have designs on her.'

'I'm vastly obliged to you for warning me. What would you suggest, if I might ask?'

'Potted plant, for the lady of the house,' said Mrs Cartwright promptly. 'Not a bunch of flowers mind, that's apt to be misunderstood sometimes. No, a nice plain pot of flowers for the window ledge.'

Jerry was feeling weak with relief at having avoided such an error. 'Do you have anything suitable?' he enquired.

'That we do, right here.'

And so it was that later that day, at a little before seven in the evening, a well-dressed young man would have been seen toiling up the hill to the Fallon place, carrying a pot of bright yellow primroses.

5

Albert Fallon was pleased to see the young man walking up the path to the house. He had heard good things about the boy and had himself been favourably impressed when he met him. Jerry Freeman had struck him as being an exceedingly modest and polite fellow. There had also been an air of restrained erudition about him, as though he knew a good deal but was not going to boast or show off his knowledge needlessly. All in all, Albert Fallon thought, this was a young man who would make the perfect husband for his headstrong daughter.

Fallon had come to Texas a little over twenty years earlier, just after the end of the War between the States. He had settled down here when Mineral Springs had been little more than a half dozen wooden huts and soddies.

Unlike most of those farming the land hereabouts, Albert Fallon had received some considerable education, but the war and subsequent 'reconstruction' of the South had so sickened him that he gave up his life in Atlanta and simply turned to farming.

It had not been a bad life and now Albert Fallon had his daughter and also, following her mother's death ten years earlier, a second wife. Maria was the current focus of his mind and he was anxious to see her married to some decent and ambitious man; a man like Jerry Freeman, perhaps.

Had he known any of this, it is very likely that Jerry would have chucked the primroses in the nearest ditch and marched straight back to his little room above the saloon. He little knew how avidly folk in a small town such as Mineral Springs followed their neighbours' business and made it their own.

'I'm very glad you could make it, Mr Freeman,' said Fallon, meeting Jerry at the door and ushering him into the house. Once inside, Jerry looked around in surprise. He had somehow thought that the farmhouse would be a rough, homely sort of place; this was as finely made and elegantly furnished as many a home he had seen in New York. To his mortification, Albert Fallon caught the look on his face and seemingly read some of his thoughts, for he said, 'Us sodbusters don't all live in mud huts and smelly dugouts, you know.'

Jerry Freeman felt himself redden, appalled to be thought of as a snob. He hardly knew what to say, but Fallon clapped him on the shoulder cheerfully and said, 'I'm only joshing, lad. Take no notice.'

Mercifully, Jerry was freed from the necessity of replying, because Maria and her stepmother came through from the kitchen. It took some believing that the young woman with Maria could possibly stand in the relation of stepmother; they looked more like sisters. Jerry thrust such thoughts from his mind, fearful that Albert Fallon would once again gauge accurately what he was thinking.

Before dinner, Fallon showed him round the house. 'Built it myself,' he said, the pride in his voice obvious. 'Started out in a soddy like everybody else, but then, by and by, I started on this place. It's built of stone and wood; it'll last a hundred years.' In another man, this might perhaps have sounded like boasting, but when Albert Fallon said it, it came across as no more than a sober and unbiased estimate of the situation.

When they were seated at the table, Fallon said grace. 'Lord, in a world where so many are hungry, we thank you that we have food to eat. In a world where so many are friendless, we thank you that we have a friend here this day to share with us in this meal. Amen.'

Once they were eating, Fallon said, 'Tell me Mr Freeman, how do you like working at The Texas Rose?'

Maria interrupted, saying, 'Lordy Pa,

'working at The Texas Rose'? Why you make it sound like he's the barkeep or something.'

'The boy knows well enough that I meant nothing of the kind,' Fallon said to his daughter. 'Hush now and let's hear what he has to say.'

'Well sir, it's hard to say. I did not plan for to be working here when I got off the train.'

'Oh,' said Fallon, simulating surprise. 'What were you planning to do when you came here?'

This was a question which many in the town had asked themselves, but Albert Fallon was the first to ask it outright. Other folk had hinted and approached the matter from a variety of indirect angles, but that was not Fallon's way. The three people at the table were looking at him as though expecting an answer and so Jerry said, 'I was running away.'

'Well, we're honoured by your confidence,' Fallon said. 'It's a rare enough man as will admit to running away. Your candour does you credit.'

'Not really,' said Jerry uncomfortably. 'It's a strange business. You see, I was running away because . . . somebody . . . wanted me to practice law in the courtroom. I didn't want that and so just jumped on to a train and, well, you know the rest.'

'So what it amounts to is this,' said Albert Fallon slowly, 'you ran away from New York so that you shouldn't have to practice law in a courtroom and ran all the way here to do that very thing. Is that how the case stands?'

'Pretty much sir, yes.'

As soon as Jerry had mentioned 'somebody' wanting him to practice law in the courtroom, Maria had been staring hard at the young attorney, knowing instinctively that 'somebody' meant a girl to whom he was close. Her father sensed this and decided that it would be tactful to change the subject, before his daughter asked outright some prying question. He said, 'But we are getting off the point, I fear. I asked you how you liked working at Judge Singer's court?'

'He certainly has an individual style of administering the law,' said Jerry tactfully, not wishing to say too much in case the Fallons turned out to be close friends of Clayton Singer.

'An individual style of administering the law,' said Fallon. 'Yes, that's one way of putting it, I suppose.' He turned to his wife and said, 'Do you recall the time that he was trying a horse thief and had his barkeep act as defence counsel?'

Mrs Fallon laughed in delight. 'It was the talk of the town for weeks. They never did catch the man, did they?'

'What happened?' asked Jerry.

'Well, this was the way of it,' said Albert Fallon. 'Before the present old fellow who acts as barkeep at The Texas Rose, there was a younger man, couldn't have been much over thirty. This was soon after Singer was appointed Justice of the Peace. Anyway, a fellow called Strong was detected in the act of stealing two ponies out at the Parkers' spread. They wanted to see him dealt with legally, so they brought him to Singer.

'Now this barkeep, he was bitterly opposed to anybody being hanged. You saw for yourself the other day, Mr Freeman, it's a dreadful business. Anyway, at that time, not long after he had been made the law for round here, Singer was a lot more particular about his trials, making sure that men had somebody to defend them. When the time came for Strong to face him, on a capital charge mind, a hanging matter, there was nobody to act for him. So Clayton, he asks the young barkeep to act as defence counsel!'

Jerry Freeman shook his head in disbelief, although from what he had seen of Clayton Singer's ways, he had no difficulty believing the story.

' 'Very well', said the barkeep, 'but if I act for him, I'll clear him.' Singer, he just tells him to get on with it. Now before Singer took to locking men in his cellar, he used to stick them in the pantry and set somebody at the door to keep a watch. On this occasion, it was Jed Parker, one of those whose horses had been stolen. He sat outside the pantry door, guarding Strong and the barkeep kept him well supplied with as much whiskey as he desired. To cut a long story short, Parker passed out and the barkeep let Strong out of the pantry and hid him in an empty whiskey barrel.

'After this, the barkeep made a speech, which was a lot of nonsense, but since Singer and the others in the saloon had been drinking themselves, that didn't signify. The judge called for the prisoner to be produced and of course, he was nowhere to be found. Whereupon, all those present commenced to drink freely and when they retired that night, drunk as . . . drunk as lords, the barkeep let Strong out and that was the last anybody ever saw of him.'

The story was greeted by gales of

laughter from all those present, which clearly pleased Fallon. Jerry asked, 'Is that really a true story?'

'You've seen a little of Clayton Singer,' said Fallon. 'What do you think?'

'I think that it sounds just exactly like him.'

Albert Fallon grew a little more serious and said, 'I'll tell you the problem, Mr Freeman, and I look to you not to retell what is said here outside this house.'

'I shouldn't dream of betraying a confidence,' said Jerry indignantly.

'Well then, here's how the matter lies. Clayton Singer is a very good saloon keeper. He always was and I've known him longer than most. But the qualities that go to make a good saloon keeper aren't always those which you might look for in a Justice of the Peace. He got that post by posting a thousand dollar bond, nothing more than that. He's had no legal training or anything of that nature.'

'I suppose,' said Jerry shrewdly,

'What you're saying is that a man who might have answered in frontier days, isn't what's needed now. You think times are changing.'

'You got it just exactly right,' said Fallon, pleased to have his meaning taken so readily. 'I'll warrant that you've not seen a character like Clayton Singer sitting on the bench in any court in New York?'

'Not hardly!' said Jerry with a smile.

'Which means that we, here in Texas, are having to make do with less than folk living in big cities in the east. It's not right. Everybody in this nation should have just the same rights under the law.'

Jerry Freeman didn't speak for a moment. What Albert Fallon was saying was all but identical to what Emma had told him. She, like this farmer in a remote area, both gauged things just the same. They both sensed that the world was changing for the better and that it was the duty of all right-thinking people to take off their jackets, roll up their sleeves and set to work to help that change come as quickly as could be.

'I think,' said Jerry, 'that you are right, sir. Maybe my duty is to help with that change.'

Fallon looked at the young man with approval. Then he said, his eyes twinkling again, 'I suppose you know that Singer is also responsible for the solemnization of marriages in this part of the county?'

'I didn't know, no, but now that you say so, it sounds reasonable.'

'He's stopped doing it now, but for the first year or two, he used to conduct the ceremony with a comic verse.'

Jerry looked at Albert Fallon aghast. 'Surely not?' he said.

'Oh yes, indeed. Would you like to hear what he used to say on the occasion?'

'I would indeed.'

'Here it is then;

Under this roof in stormy weather,
The buck and squaw now come
together,

Let not but *Him* who rules the
thunder,
Pull this buck and squaw asunder,
I now pronounce you man and
wife,
And may God have mercy on your
souls,
Now, what's your pleasure?

Everybody fairly fell about laughing at this. Jerry asked, 'Tell me now, did he truly use those words to conduct weddings?'

'That he did,' replied Fallon, 'And being the duly authorized Justice of the Peace that he is, the marriages earned out in that way were legally binding.'

As he walked home at about ten that night, Jerry Freeman reflected that this had been the most agreeable time that he had had since leaving New York. Albert Fallon was a good natured and entertaining man and his wife was good company too. As for Maria . . .

Jerry didn't rightly know how he felt about Maria Fallon. She was lively and quick-witted and stimulating to be with, but he didn't think that he was about to fall in love with her in a hurry. All other considerations apart, he was still longing for Emma and didn't see that passing in the near future. Lost in these thoughts, Jerry almost bumped into a man who appeared to be dawdling around in his path. 'I do beg your pardon,' said Jerry. 'I didn't see you there.'

'No harm done,' said the man, 'M'name's Crawford, Clint Crawford. Hey, would I be right in thinkin' you're the lawyer? Mr Freeman?'

'Yes, I am,' said Jerry, moving to one side, to let the man pass.

Clint Crawford gave no indication that he was planning to move. Instead, he said: 'Well now, that's a coincidence that I should o' banged into you here.'

'Coincidence?' asked Jerry. 'How so?' It was only later, when he was tucked up in his bed that it dawned on him that there had been no coincidence in the case and that Crawford had been hanging around between the Fallon place and The Texas Rose with the express purpose of speaking to him.

'It's like this,' said the man. 'I got a bit of a question as touches 'pon the law.'

Although inwardly, he gave a sigh, Jerry didn't show that he was just wanting to get to his bed. Instead, he said to Crawford, 'Would you like to come up to The Texas Rose? We could talk about it more comfortably there.'

'That's a mite awkward. I'd sooner talk here if it's the same to you.'

'All right then. Why don't we walk along as we talk? It's a little chilly to stand still for long.'

The two of them began to amble around the perimeter of Mineral Springs and Clint Crawford revealed what was on his mind.

'It's like this, Mr Freeman. I own a parcel o' land over yonder, t'other side of the railroad tracks. Now I got it in mind to build a little place there, nothing fancy. Somewhere that those who are waiting while the trains take on water could buy somewhat to eat and drink, if they was so minded.'

'That sounds a right smart move,' said Jerry. 'From what I've seen, you would be sure to do a roaring trade. What's the problem? Why do you seek my advice?'

'I'm afeared as Judge Singer wouldn't take to the notion.'

'I can't see that it would be any affair of his. You say you own the land?'

'Oh yes,' said Crawford. 'I own a heap of the land over on that side.'

'Then I can't see that anybody could object. It would be healthy competition for The Texas Rose and with the two of you vying for custom, I guess it would have the effect of making both establishments keen to maintain their standards.'

'So you see no lawful reason as why I shouldn't do it?'

'None in the world. I wish you every success.'

Jerry Freeman more or less forgot

about this conversation as soon as he parted from Clint Crawford and the next day, he hardly recollected it at all.

Judge Singer was keen to speak to Jerry, first thing the following morning. The barkeep rapped on his door at about eight and said, 'Judge Singer sends his compliments and would be pleased to breakfast with you.' After hastily throwing on his clothes and not stopping to shave or even brush his hair, Jerry hurried down to the bar-room. Singer was sitting at a table with a cup of coffee and said, as soon as he caught sight of the attorney, 'You took your time. Come here now, I've something to talk over with you.'

Once Jerry had settled himself down with a coffee and slice of bread, Singer launched straight into what he had to say. 'Fact is, young feller, you're good for business. Not just here, but for everybody in town. Takin's was good in the store and smithy, as well as this place.'

'I dare say that the hanging was an

attraction,' said Jerry coldly.

Judge Singer didn't appear to notice the sarcastic tone in which this was said, but continued, 'Yeah, you got it just right. But it ain't just hanging's as I'm thinkin' 'bout. You ever been to some town on Court Day?'

'I can't say that I have, no.'

'Well everybody goes there from miles around. It's like a carnival or somethin' has come to town. Sometimes folk set up market stalls, you know, sellin' food and such. And like you say, hangings, well they're something else again. Why it's a regular festival on hangin' days.'

Jerry Freeman shot his patron a look of undisguised scorn. He said, 'What would you have, a bunch of executions to boost trade in Mineral Springs.'

This time, Singer did pick up on Jerry's tone and he said, 'You're a snot-nosed one all right. Still and all, you and me need each other, I reckon. Doesn't mean we got to like each other over-much though.'

'What is it that you want of me?'

'Now we're talkin'. I want to build up Court Day here so that it's a big draw. Hangin's too, maybe. We could even aim to have folks visitin' by railroad. Only thing is, we'd need to have a few changes.'

'What sort of changes?' asked Jerry, curious in spite of his distaste for Singer's enthusiasm about hangings as a mean to bring in customers for his saloon.

'Well now, a proper courtroom for one. We couldn't have us a Court Day every Monday afternoon, like we do now. We'd need to have it once a month, but make a real big show of it. Might need a cell too, you know, somewhere to hold prisoners and such.'

'Yes, I know what a cell is.'

Singer stopped talking and waited to hear the attorney's response to his ideas. Now repugnant as was Clayton Singer's keenness to see people flocking to a hanging, there was still something wholesome and good about the notion of having a courtroom, rather than seeing man sentenced to death in a saloon. Singer's motives were disgusting enough and yet his aim could work to the benefit of civilization. Even the idea of having proper cells, instead of tying up a man and thrusting him into a dark cellar, was a good one.

'Well,' said Singer impatiently. 'What d'you say? Will you lend a hand?'

'I don't see why not.'

6

The place which Clayton Singer had in mind for his new courtroom was an old barn which stood on the edge of town. Originally, this patch of land had been part of a smallholding, but Mineral Springs had expanded and slowly but surely, the little farm had been squeezed out of existence. All that now remained was the barn. Jerry went with Singer to look over the place after breakfast.

There were several advantages from the point of view of converting this place into a courthouse. One was that it had what could easily be converted into a cell. After the farm had been swallowed up by the town, a man had rented this barn as a livery stable. He had constructed an office inside, which was very stoutly made. With a few additional precautions, this little room could become a holding cell.

'It will need a good deal of work to get it looking presentable,' remarked Jerry.

'Was thinkin' the self-same thing myself,' said Judge Singer. 'You ain't got any objection to working with a hammer and saw, I s'pose?'

'I haven't done a lot of work with my hands,' replied Jerry, 'but I'm happy to start now.'

'That's the boy. We'll have it ready in no time.'

Jerry Freeman thought that Singer was being wildly optimistic if he thought for a moment that the dusty old barn would be ready for use in much under a month, but the old man was surprisingly energetic when the mood took him and when there was a strong business end to some enterprise.

From some farmer who owed him a favour, Singer obtained a wagon load of lumber. It was all decent wood, although of varying sizes and shapes.

He had this delivered and stored in the barn. Then he sat down with Jerry and worked out what their courthouse should look like inside. As Singer said, 'We can fuss about a lick o' paint on the outside, later. That don't signify to start with.'

Both men agreed that a raised platform was needed, from which the judge would preside over the court. There would need to be benches for the public as well. Judge Singer referred to these as the 'audience', but Jerry pointed out that this was not perhaps the best way of describing those who had come to see justice dispensed. There would also have to be a dock, for the prisoner to sit in and a few other things.

'What about tables and so on?' asked Jerry.

'Don't fret none about them,' said Singer. 'I can get them no difficulty. The minister at the church owes me a favour too, he'll lend his pews, long as it's not on a Sunday.'

When Jerry had told Judge Singer that he hadn't done a lot of work with his hands, he was understating the case to a not inconsiderable degree; truth was, he had never so much as handled a hammer or saw in the whole course of his life. He had never had need to do so. After all he wasn't aiming to become a carpenter. His mother and father had made sure that their precious only child never needed to get his hands soiled by labouring with them.

All of which meant that by the end of the first day, Jerry's hands were covered with blisters. Singer had got a few more men to help out and when they noticed the blisters on the lawyer's hands, they laughed and teased him. Jerry took all this in good part and the next day, he was back again, hammering and sawing, fetching and carrying. Maria passed him while he was moving a pile of planks about, one by one, and she stopped to chat to him.

'My father wants me to ask you to

visit again. But only if you want to come.'

'Are they your words or his?' asked Jerry.

'He asked me to invite you, but I don't want you to come unless you wish to.'

He smiled at her and said, 'I'd be pleased to come by your house again, but I can't stop now to talk. Let's make plans when I'm free.'

The girl shrugged indifferently, as though it were a matter of small consequence to her whether Jerry Freeman came to her house or not. She was vexed, because the young man had made no sort of advance to her and for all she knew to the contrary, he had agreed to come and visit again because he hoped to see her father, rather than her.

Jerry himself knew nothing of these doubts going through Maria Fallon's head and simply recognized that she was being a little cold and formal to him.

It took two weeks to get the old barn into some sort of condition that might be fit for visitors. It still looked mighty rough, but at least when you peered through that door, you could see at a glance that this was no common barn. You might not have been able to guess its real purpose, but you could see at once that this wasn't a place used to stable horses or store bales of hay.

'What say we have the next court session here?' Singer said on the Saturday that they finally used up all the lumber and had swept the place out.

'I can't see why not,' said Jerry. 'It will at any rate be an improvement on the saloon.'

'Ah, that's served well enough. But I mind as Mineral Springs is going to be on the map soon and I want folks coming here to find a real town.'

'There's more to a town than it being somewhere with a courthouse,' said Jerry.

'It's a start,' replied Judge Singer,

which, thought Jerry Freeman, was indisputably true.

Now if things had carried on in this way, it is altogether possible that Jerry might have stayed on in Mineral Springs and even graduated to being the next judge. He might perhaps have married Maria and settled down in Texas and in time the memory of Emma would have faded and he would have been quite content. There are a thousand maybes and might-have-beens like this in everybody's life. What actually happened was that within two weeks of that courtroom being built and ready for action, Jerry Freeman was on the run from Mineral Springs and wanted for a capital crime.

Things began to unravel for Jerry's life in the little town, on the Monday morning after finishing the new court. Judge Singer was in a bad mood, because there was nobody to try that afternoon, nor any other business like marriages or property disputes to settle and he was afraid that people would feel let down and cheated if they came to town and there was no show. Singer's temper wasn't improved at all when he noticed signs of activity over by the railroad tracks. It looked to him as though somebody was building something near the line, an idea that was absolute anathema to the saloon keeper. When he wandered down to see what was what, it was to find Clint Crawford, of all people, setting up a stall to sell refreshments to those passengers who had ten minutes to spare when the locomotive stopped to take on water. Never one to mince his words or put off unpleasantness, Singer crossed the tracks and asked Crawford just what the hell he thought he was about.

'I'm setting up a little store here,' said Crawford. 'No law against it.'

'No law against it,' said Singer wrathfully. 'No law against it? We'll see 'bout that.' Then he received news of what he viewed as rank treachery on the part of the man who to his mind was beholden to him, because Crawford continued:

'Your man says as it's all legal and above board.'

'My man? Who you talkin' about?'

'Young Freeman. I asked him last week and he told me I could go right ahead.'

'You'd do well to knock down this pile o' shit now,' said Singer, 'and that's all I got to say on the subject. Don't let me see this thing here tomorrow.'

It has to be said that Judge Singer was probably making altogether too much fuss about Clint Crawford's little enterprise. The structure that he was throwing up alongside the railroad tracks was really nothing more than a booth, for all that he was describing it as a 'store'. It looked as though when finished, it would not be more than say six feet by ten; a little wooden hut with one large window with a shelf at front. This modest wooden box though was more than Singer was aiming to put up with.

* * *

At about the same time that Monday morning that Clayton Singer went off angrily in search of his Public Defender, Albert Fallon was talking amiably to a drifter who had stopped to beg a cup of water. This man, who called himself Dave Travis, was a pleasant, open-faced young man in his mid-twenties. He was well spoken, which was unusual in the hobos and drifters who passed through Mineral Springs from time to time. Fallon took to him, the fellow seemed to him like a gentleman fallen on hard times, and when Travis asked if he knew of any work going in the district, Albert Fallon did not hesitate to say, 'Well, if you can handle an axe, I might have a day or two's labouring for you. Mind, I'll need to see how you can do for an hour or two first.'

'Why, that's right nice of you,' said Travis, his face splitting in a wide smile. 'I don't reckon you need worry about my strength or endurance, when it comes to hard work.'

Travis proved to be no idle boaster and Fallon was astonished at the amount of wood that the slim young man was able to chop in an hour. He looked a lazy, good-natured but slightly languid type, but he surely could work. The result was that after a couple of hours, Fallon said to him, 'Come in the house now for something to eat and we'll talk things over.' Already, Fallon had more than half decided to ask the man if he wanted to stay around for a few days, perhaps sleeping in the barn.

* * *

Judge Singer found Jerry in the new courtroom, sanding down some rough edges on a rail, so that people might not run the risk of getting splinters when they brushed against it. Singer wasn't one to waste words, especially when he was as riled up as he was right then.

'What the hell you playin' at, Freeman?'

'Me? I'm getting your new court ready. What's wrong?'

'You tell that skunk Crawford as he could set up in opposition to me?'

'I truly have not the least idea what you are talking about,' said Jerry Freeman. 'Would you care to explain?'

'Never mind your fancy talk, it won't answer now. Did you tell Clint Crawford as he could open a store up by the railroad?'

'Oh, that.'

'Yeah, that. What d'you say to him?'

'I said that if he owned the land, I couldn't see why he shouldn't build on it. No more than that. Why?'

' 'Cause the bastard's fixin' to sell drinks to the folk on trains, that's why.'

Jerry considered this for a moment and then said, 'Surely there's room for two places in town to buy drinks?'

'You got that wrong. There ain't. Anybody wants a drink, they come to The Texas Rose.'

Jerry shook his head in disbelief.

'Judge, the town is growing. Even I can see it and I haven't been here above five minutes. What happens when you have a thousand people living here or ten thousand? Are they all going to have to come to your saloon if they want a drink?'

'Long as I've got breath in my body they will, yes.'

Singer turned on his heel and left the barn. Jerry could tell that he was exceedingly irate about the business and his anger was probably directed evenly between Crawford and him. It was just one more small example of the way that the town's development and progress was being hampered by one powerful man. In the long run of course, Clayton Singer would be swept away by that progress or he would die and the problem would be resolved in that way. But for now, it was plain that Singer was the roadblock which was stopping Mineral Springs from catching up with the more civilized parts of the country. There really was something positively feudal about the way he ran the town.

* * *

Maria was impressed with the man who her father had invited to share their midday meal. He was handsome, young and spoke beautifully, even better than Jerry Freeman. And this man, unlike Jerry, seemed to take notice of her as a woman. It was indefinable and she was too modest a young woman to have put it into words, even to herself, but she knew that Dave Travis had noted her face and body and was pleased with what he saw. Jerry Freeman was polite and friendly as you like, but at the same time, Maria was aware that he didn't think of her in *that* way. There was no doubt though that Travis did think of her like that. A couple of times during the meal, she glanced up to find his eyes upon her and not only on her face either! Travis saw that she had caught him staring at her and when their eyes met, rather than looking away, embarrassed, he smiled at her roguishly. She hoped that her father would be asking this fellow to stay around for a while.

That afternoon, Maria had to walk into town to get some provisions. On Main Street, she saw Jerry Freeman walking towards her and when he caught sight of her, he smiled in the friendliest way imaginable, as though he were really pleased to see her. But friendship was all she *did* see in that smile of his and she had a suspicion that the attorney was never going to see her as anything other than that; just a friend. Nevertheless, she smiled back and they stopped to chat.

'Do you want to come and see the new courtroom?' asked Jerry proudly.

'Oh, I heard about that. Yes, show me it.'

They walked towards the old barn and Jerry said, 'I was hoping I'd see you again soon.'

'Were you? Why?'

'It's good to see a friendly face. I think most people in town see me like the minister or something, just one of those men that you are polite to and use from time to time, but don't specially want as a friend.'

'Is that what I am to you, a friend?'

'Well I certainly hope so. Why, are we not friends?'

'Yes, don't fret. We're friends all right.'

When she saw the inside of the old barn, Maria had to make a conscious effort not to burst out laughing. Jerry was so clearly proud of the place and pointed out where the judge and public would sit and suchlike. Unfortunately, he saw her lips twitching and said, offended, 'What's so funny?'

She couldn't help it then, but just started giggling like a little girl. 'What is it?' asked Jerry again and she felt ashamed for laughing at something which was obviously a source of pride to him.

'I'm sorry,' said Maria, 'but this place

reminds me of something and it isn't a courtroom?'

'What then?'

'My father took me to the county seat a while back. He wanted to attend an auction there and it was held in a special place. This looks just like it! The auctioneer sat up on a raised platform and all us that were doing the bidding were in a space like this here. What you got here isn't a courtroom at all, it's an auction room.' She was overcome with laughter again and said, 'I have to go to the store. It was nice seeing you.'

As she walked to the store, Maria was thinking to herself that there really was something a littie ridiculous about Jerry Freeman. Standing there so proud of that old barn! And his face, so good natured and eager. Unbidden, the memory of Dave Travis looking appreciatively at her body came to her and she flushed slightly. Now there was a man who had noticed her the moment he set eyes upon her!

Jerry stood looking after the girl as

she headed down Main Street to the store. There was something a mite puzzling about her today, but he couldn't make out what it was.

There were more people in town that Monday than was usual. Word about the hanging and the exciting trial which had preceded it had spread around the district and just as Singer had hoped, was having the effect of drawing people to Mineral Springs. It was vexing that there was nobody to put on trial this afternoon. Truth to tell, he would have been pleased to see that young devil Freeman on trial and maybe dangling at the end of the rope afterwards, but then his performances in court were part of the attraction which Judge Singer was promoting. Without the New York lawyer, the trials in Mineral Springs would provide no more than the occasional footnote in newspapers. What he really needed to put the town on the map was a big murder trial with the killer ably defended by Jerry Freeman and ending with a hanging.

When, on Monday night, Clint Crawford's hut for selling refreshments to thirsty railroad passengers burned to the ground, Jerry for one knew at once who had been behind the arson. He also knew that Clayton Singer would have been too cunning either to carry out such an act himself or to allow it to be traced back to him. That being so, he saw no point in worrying about it. A judge conspiring to commit arson, indeed! He had never heard anything like it.

With a very bad grace, Judge Singer decided that there was no point opening up the new court and inviting the public in until there were a few criminals to try. He was also beginning to wonder about the sense in letting that awkward young devil continue to eat his head off at Singer's expense and carry on living in his saloon. Both these problems were solved a week later in the most surprising manner imaginable.

* * *

Dave Travis stayed on at the Fallons' farm and unrolled his blanket in the barn each night. He was a good worker and Albert Fallon was happy to provide him with his meals and a few dollars over. He could see also that Maria was taken with the fellow, but didn't much trouble about that. He was secretly betting on her and Jerry Freeman getting hitched up in the fullness of time and if the girl wished to flirt lightly with the hired help until then, well it did nobody any harm.

After he had finished work for the day and before the evening meal, Travis was at a loose end and Maria took to coming out to chat with him while he was tidying up and putting away the tools which he had been using. On the early evening of Tuesday, April 30th 1889, Travis asked Maria Fallon if she would care to walk with him out into the hills behind her home. Her father had no objection, provided that they were back in time for dinner and so the two of them set off at around half past five and were last seen walking, side by side, along the track which led north into the hills.

When the young couple were not back after a couple of hours, Albert Fallon began to grow distinctly uneasy. He checked the clock every few minutes, until his wife suggested that he ride after Maria and the hired man and see what was delaying them. Fallon didn't like to do this, as he thought it might look as though he were spying on his daughter or didn't trust her or something of that sort. He waited until the clock struck eight and then went outside. There was still no sign of Maria and Dave Travis and he knew that something had happened. Please God that it was only that the child had sprained her ankle or some trifling matter like that. As the sun was setting, Fallon was about to tack up his horse when he saw in the distance a sight which sent a chill through his whole being. Running and staggering towards him along that same track up which his daughter and Travis had gone nearly three hours earlier, a single figure was heading. Fallon ran forwards and soon realized that this was Travis.

The running man looked to be in a pitiful condition, with blood running down his face. As Albert Fallon came nigh to him, he could hear the man panting, wheezing and crying.

'Travis, what in God's name has happened,' cried the farmer. 'Where's my daughter?'

'We were jumped.'

'Jumped? What the hell are you talking of, jumped?'

Travis sank to the ground in exhaustion. He said, 'We were out about a mile on from here. Two men rode up and were . . . well, rude to Maria. I reproved them and they got down from their horses. We had a fearful set-to and they beat me senseless. When I came to, just a few minutes since, I found the men had gone and your daughter was . . . laying there.'

'Mother of God man, is she all right? Say she's not too badly hurt.'

'I'm so sorry, Mr Fallon. I checked her over at once. I'm afraid they've done for her. She's dead.'

7

When he heard about the murder of Albert Fallon's daughter, Singer was man enough to feel grieved for the fellow's loss. The girl's stepmother came running into town, almost hysterical, within an hour of the crime coming to light. But after this decent emotion had passed, Judge Singer began to plan how he could make capital of the crime. This would surely be one of the most sensational trials ever held in Mineral Springs. What a mercy that he had thought to set up that new courtroom!

Once Singer had the facts of the case, he didn't hesitate in what he conceived as his duty. It was late at night, but he rounded up a few former members of the vigilance committee and they all rode out together to the Fallon place. Six or seven years ago, they would have been carrying a rope and been keeping an eye out for a handy, nearby tree, but now the aim was to bring the Fallons' hired man back to town and lock him in the newly built cell until they could work out whether or not he had been responsible for such an atrocious crime.

Albert Fallon had been struck all of a heap by the discovery of his daughter's corpse. Travis had been a tower of strength. Despite his own injuries, he helped bring the dead girl back to the house and lay her out on the kitchen table. Mrs Fallon had then gone to town to tell what had happened. When Judge Singer and his men arrived, it was to find Travis comforting the Fallons and doing his best to help. Albert Fallon was barely coherent, so grief stricken was he, but he managed to invite Singer into the house. He pointed at the table, saying, 'See what they did to my little girl!'

'We'll talk about this tomorrow, Albert,' said Singer. 'In the meantime we've come for your man.'

'My man?' said Fallon, 'What do you want with him?'

'Need to ask him some questions is all. Shouldn't take too long.'

'Can't it wait to morning? He's been a comfort to us.'

'Can't be done. He's a-got to be comin' with us this very minute.'

Once the little group were on the track to town, with Dave Travis walking in the midst of the five riders, Singer told him, 'You'll hang for this, you bastard. Don't bother tryin' to sweet talk me or nothin'.'

* * *

The next day, Mineral Springs was seething with indignation about the terrible murder. It was rumoured that the dead girl had been raped and this made the whole affair ten times more shocking. The fact that a drifter who had only arrived in the area a week before was now sitting in a cell meant only one thing to most of the folk in town: that the killer had been caught and would, in due cause, hang for his crime.

Jerry Freeman had heard a lot of coming and going as he lay in bed on Tuesday night, but it wasn't until he came down for his breakfast that he learned the horrifying details of what had happened the day before. The old barkeep was grimly satisfied that justice would be done. 'Mr Singer's goin' to make a big show of this case,' he told Jerry. 'Let people know what happens to filthy devils like that.'

'But is it certain that this fellow was to blame?' asked the attorney innocently.

'He was out walkin' with her, from what I hear. Then come back and she was dead and'd been molested. It's plain enough.'

'Where's Judge Singer now?'

'He's down by the railroad.' It was on the tip of Jerry Freeman's tongue to ask whether Singer was down there setting fire to something else, but he thought that might not be the smartest thing to say under the circumstances. He chose instead to gulp down a quick cup of coffee and head over to find Singer.

A train had just pulled in and the crew were filling the locomotive with water. A stampede of passengers passed Jerry, heading towards The Texas Rose in order to buy beer or something to eat. He saw Singer, talking urgently to the uniformed guard from the van at the back of the train. The saloon owner looked to Jerry to be up to no good and he saw him slip a folded bill to the guard. When he spotted the attorney, Singer looked irritated and not a little guilty.

'What's going on?' asked Jerry, when he was a little closer.

'None of your business,' said Singer. 'What are you about, snoopin' round like this?'

'You bribing that man to do something?'

It was plain that Judge Singer wanted to tell Jerry to get to the devil and mind his own affairs, but he probably guessed that this would just arouse the young man's curiosity even further. So he said, 'It's nothin', just sending out some invitations.'

'Invitations?' said Jerry. 'My God, you're touting this murder to newspapers, aren't you?'

'An' what if I am? I'm putting us on the map.'

'What are you after, big crowds for the trial?'

'Somethin' like that. Anyways, what for are you botherin' me here? Don't you think you ought to be speakin' to your client?'

'Yes, I heard that you have the Fallons' hired man locked up. Can I go see him?'

'Sure, that's what your job is, ain't it? You cut along now.'

Jerry was carrying his own burden of guilt that morning, which was perhaps why he hadn't displayed more outrage at Clayton Singer's plans to turn a forthcoming murder trial into a three ring circus. It was absurd, but Jerry felt guilty that he was not more upset by hearing of Maria's death. Of course, he was sorry about it and thought it a dreadful business, but he wasn't grief-stricken. In fact, he was no more disturbed, than if the victim of the crime had been a complete stranger and he had read about it in the newspaper. Surely that wasn't right? By the time that he got to the barn where he had helped construct a secure cell, Jerry was minded to consider himself almost as blameworthy as the man who had beaten Maria Fallon to death.

Some crony of Singer's was sitting guard outside the cell, which was really the old office of the livery stable, only greatly strengthened and with the addition of a stout door, with a little barred window in it. When the man saw Jerry coming, he stood up and said, 'Morning, Mr Freeman. I'm guessing you'll want to speak to yon fellow?'

'Yes please, Judge Singer said it would be all right.'

'You'll have to go in there with him and I'll lock the door behind you. That all right?'

'Sure.'

It was the first time that Jerry had actually spoken to the hired man from the Fallons' farm. He had seen him at a distance one day last week, when he had come to the store for something or other for Mrs Fallon, but that was all.

When Jerry entered the cell, the prisoner stood up and put out his hand, saying, 'David Travis. How do you do?'

Acting instinctively, Jerry shook hands with Travis and said, 'Jerry Freeman. How do you do?' They might have been meeting in a church, the whole thing was that natural and respectable. 'If this comes to trial, Mr Travis, I'll be defending you. Perhaps you could tell me what happened?'

There was only room for a bed in the poky little cell and so the two of them sat, side by side, as Dave Travis told his story.

'Maria and I went for a walk, up into

the hills,' he began, and at once, Jerry Freeman identified with the other man. Most people in Mineral Springs would have said, 'Me and Maria', but this man had been brought up to be very careful about using grammatically correct language. This created a sense of affinity between them from the beginning. Without even noticing, Jerry began to believe Travis, even before hearing what he had to say. 'We got a mile or two and were just about to turn back, when a couple of riders came up to us.'

'From which direction?'

'From ahead of us, north.'

'Go on.'

'One of them made a coarse remark about Maria, I can't repeat it. I told him to watch his mouth and then he and his partner took exception. They got down from their horses and set upon me. I don't like to boast, but I can handle myself well enough in a fight. Had they fought fair, I'm sure I could have beaten them, but I knocked one down and then when I turned my attentions to his friend, I think he must have lamped me from behind. I guess they knocked me about while I was unconscious, because when I came to, I was pretty beat up and bruised.'

Jerry looked closely at the other man's face. It was true that he looked as though he had been in the wars a bit.

'When I came to, I was laying on the ground, next to Maria. She had been knocked about too. She was dead.'

'Is that it?'

'Pretty well. Her clothes were disarranged. I pulled her skirts down a little, to make her look more decent and then I tried to find a pulse. There was nothing. She was dead.'

'So who says that you were responsible? Did Albert Fallon accuse you?'

'No, not a bit of it! He protested last night when they brought me here. He doesn't think I had anything to do with it.'

'I don't get it. Who's saying that you killed the girl?'

Travis shrugged. 'On the way here,

some old man called me a bastard and said I'd hang.'

Everything became clear and Jerry Freeman's heart sank. Whether he really believed David Travis to be guilty or not, and to be fair to the man it was possible that he genuinely thought it to be the case, Clayton Singer was determined to have a grand trial in his new courthouse, culminating presumably with the hanging of the man sitting next to him.

Jerry said, 'Look, I know it's hard, but try not to worry too much. I'm going to get you out of here if I can.'

'Gee, I hope so. I've never been in any sort of trouble in my life. This is a terrible thing. That poor girl. And Mr Fallon, I don't know how he'll bear this. He was that devoted to his daughter.'

After leaving Dave Travis, the young attorney went straight off in search of the judge. He found him at The Texas Rose and Jerry didn't mince his words. 'What evidence is there against that man you've got locked up?'

'He went out with Fallon's daughter and she was raped and murdered. What more d'you want?'

'But he's been hurt himself!' protested Jerry.

Singer looked at him queerly. He said, 'You been on the earth as long as me son, you'd know as men lie about everything and that oftentimes, they can't control themselves, once they get excited about a woman. I'd say he hit himself a few dines on his forehead with a rock. Cunning, I grant you, but you got to get up a sight earlier in the day to put one over on me. I tell you, he's guilty as Cain.'

'This is crazy! Have you been to look at where he says this happened?'

'No need. I'm tellin' you he did it.'

* * *

Jerry wasn't at all sure what sort of reception he might expect to receive from Albert Fallon. The door was opened not by either Fallon or his wife, but by a neighbour who was sitting with the family. There were a half dozen people in the house, who had come by to condole with the Fallons. Maria's body had been laid out in another room. When Albert Fallon caught sight of Jerry, he went up to him and greeted him in a tired and listless way.

'Good of you to come,' he mumbled and Jerry could only mutter something trite about being sorry for his loss. He certainly could not bring himself to question the man about the circumstances of his daughter's death. After staying for as short a time as still seemed decent and fitting, he left and headed up into the hills, to see what he could find.

Perhaps a mile and a half from the Fallon's house, a little off the track, Jerry found what he was looking for. A trail of footprints led off the track to one side, presumably made by those who had come up here in the darkness and picked up Maria Fallon and brought home her lifeless body. Who had done that, he wondered? Was it Albert Fallon and David Travis? He examined the ground nearby and could see what looked to him to be the signs of scuffing, as though there had been a struggle, with at least two people kicking their feet around. Maybe some Indian scout could have read what had taken place here, but it was beyond him. He walked back to town, more determined than ever in his own mind that an innocent man was sitting in that cell and that unless he, Jerry Freeman, acted, that man would hang next Monday.

For the next week, the attorney worked hard at preparing a defence for the man he believed was being held unjustly for the murder of Maria Fallon. Although Singer was definitely delighted to be able to stage a murder trial in the new court, Jerry had the charity to see that the man really believed Travis guilty of the crime. It might accord with Clayton Singer's ideas for increasing the prosperity of

Mineral Springs, but at the same time, he was convinced that he would be undertaking a laudable public service in ridding the world of a man he viewed as being on a par with a mad dog who needed to be destroyed.

What chiefly worried Jerry Freeman was that there was not a scrap of evidence to show either that Travis had committed the dreadful crime or that he was lying in his account of what had taken place that day. He saw Travis twice a day and found that he had an affinity with the man; they were very similar in many ways. After he had explained how he came to be working as the public defender in a small place like Mineral Springs, Travis bashfully admitted that he was in a similar case and that he too was roaming the country in the wake of a wrecked love affair. He gave no details, but Jerry understood there to be a tragic flavour to the business which was lacking in his own case.

Try as he might, Jerry was unable to

get Singer to agree to any sort of postponement. He was utterly determined that the trial should go ahead a little less than a week after the murder. Jerry guessed that the judge had, in effect, sent out word to nearby towns that they would be sure of a good entertainment if they came to the trial.

Monday dawned bright and clear. Just as when he was holding trials in The Texas Rose, Judge Singer intended to start Dave Travis's trial at half past two in the afternoon. This, he calculated, would ensure that those coming to town to watch the trial and witness the execution would spend half a day spending money in his saloon and anywhere else in Mineral Springs.

By midday, the little town was heaving with visitors. Some of these arrived by train, stopping off in Mineral Springs from one train and then planning to either continue their journey or return home by another. Whatever methods Singer had used to spread the word had been remarkably effective. At this rate, it would be standing room only in the courtroom when the trial began that afternoon.

At eleven, Jerry went to visit his client one final time. Travis' pleasant and open face looked completely untroubled by the ordeal which he faced. If I were in his shoes, thought Jerry to himself, I'd be sweating blood. Probably, Travis did not fully understand that he was going to be appearing in a courtroom where the judge was also the prosecuting counsel and the jury would bring in a verdict of guilty just so as not to annoy the fellow who ran the saloon which they patronized. Perhaps it was just as well that Dave Travis didn't know any of this.

'How are you feeling?' asked Jerry sympathetically.

'Oh you know. A mite nervous, but nothing to speak of. I know I've done nothing wrong and I'm sure that the jury will see that. You'll see, we'll be drinking together in the saloon tonight.'

This was such an optimistic rendering of the situation, that Jerry sneaked a closer look at the man he would be defending. It was almost as though he didn't fully appreciate that he would be on trial for his life in a few hours. For all that he was a man standing in the shadow of the noose, David Travis might have been talking about a visit to the dentist.

'I'll see you this afternoon then,' said Jerry uncomfortably. 'Try not to worry. I'll do my best for you.'

As he strolled along Main Street, Jerry Freeman tried to make some sense of Travis' cheerful demeanour. Didn't he know that there was an excellent chance that by tonight, he would be dead? Of course, it was a mercy that he didn't understand the peril that he was in, but all the same it was blazing strange. There was a puzzle here that he could not quite figure out and yet he was sure that it had some bearing upon the case against the fellow.

Back at The Texas Rose, the saloon was full to bursting' and Jerry didn't rate his chances too highly of getting served a meal. He retraced his steps to the general store, to buy some bread and cheese. Mrs Cartwright was behind the counter and she was pleased to see Jerry.

'Mind you do your best for that fellow as is setting in that cell,' was her greeting. 'Jane Fallon came by here yesterday and she was distraught. Says Albert has barely touched a morsel since his daughter died.'

'What do they think about this business? Do they think that Mr Travis did it?'

'Not a bit of it. Jane said that he was a regular gentleman. Says she'd take oath that he had no hand in the matter.'

It was while he was eating his bread and cheese outside, leaning against a wall in the sun, that Jerry Freeman knew that he would have to do anything at all to save that man's life. It was one of those times that he had heard of, when everything depended upon one person and life and death hung in the balance. He could not, would not, be found wanting.

His talks with Travis had given Jerry Freeman some solid ideas for his defence. He also had one or two surprises in his pocket: surprises which would rely for their effectiveness upon Clayton Singer's own actions. With a bit of luck, the saloon owner would find himself hoist with his own petard this afternoon.

In a little notebook, the attorney had jotted down the details which Dave Travis had given him about his previous life. That a man such as he would simply rape and beat to death the daughter of the man on whose property he was staying, somebody at whose table he had been eating for a week, defied all reason. Then again, surely he would have known that he would be the first suspect in such an event as this. None of it made any sort of sense. He consulted his pocket watch: a gift from his father on his twenty-first birthday. It lacked only a quarter hour before the trial began. He had better make tracks and prepare himself. This might be a gruelling experience.

8

As Jerry Freeman had guessed, all the seats in the court were taken and there were any number of people standing at the back. Singer had arranged with the church to borrow their benches for the day, having sworn that he would ensure that none were damaged or marked at all by the spectators in his court. Proceedings began with the swearing in of the jury, all of whom lived in or near to Mineral Springs and consequently knew the dead girl and her father. When Travis was brought from his cell to stand in the dock, all twelve of these men gazed coldly at him. It was pretty plain that they had already made up their minds. He recalled a visit he had made to a New York court and a conversation he had overheard between two men who had been summoned for jury service. One had said, 'I ask myself when I look at the fellow in the dock, if he hasn't done anything wrong, what's he doing here?' The man to whom he spoke had nodded vigorously; this made perfect sense to him.

Judge Singer opened the case by outlining the events of that fatal night. It was still an extraordinary thing for Jerry to watch a judge acting as prosecuting counsel in this way, but there was little enough he was able to do about it. He could only try and sway the jury and hope that they would find his arguments convincing.

Having outlined the crime of which the man in the dock was accused, Judge Singer called the first witness, the dead girl's father.

Albert Fallon looked like a wraith and Jerry was dreading the idea of having to cross-examine him. All other considerations apart, being the least bit rough or demanding with this poor man would be sure to prejudice the jury against him, and by association, his client.

After being sworn in, Fallon told the court how he had met Travis coming back that night and how they had then gone back to look for Maria. On finding her, they had carried the body of the slight girl back to Fallon's house.

'See any sign of anyone, 'part from Travis?' asked Judge Singer.

'No, nobody.'

'Did the 'cused have blood on his clothing?'

'He did.'

'Your witness, Mr Freeman.'

Jerry stood up and asked quietly, 'Mr Fallon, do you think that David Travis killed your daughter?'

Before Fallon had a chance to reply, Judge Singer hollered out: 'Don't answer that question! It's for the jury to decide who killed Maria Fallon. How long'd you known Travis, Mr Fallon?'

'At the time of . . . you mean when . . . '

'Yes, yes,' said Singer hastily, 'At that time, how long?'

'About a week, I guess.'

'There y'are, Freeman,' said Singer. 'Mr Fallon didn't know the man well enough to know what he might o' been capable of. We'd need to speak to folk as has knowed him all his life, if we want to know what sort o' man he is and if he'd be likely to commit murder.'

Under his breath, Jerry muttered, 'The Lord hath delivered him into mine hands!' He could hardly believe his luck. Out loud he said meekly, 'Just as your honour pleases. Mr Fallon, do you know why Mr Travis had blood on his clothes?'

'Yes, his head was all beat up. He had blood running down his face from where he had been attacked . . . '

Judge Singer cut in, saying, 'We goin' to hear evidence of the accused directly. Thank you Mr Fallon. No further questions?'

Jerry shook his head. He was not at all sanguine about the chance of securing an acquittal of the man who he firmly believed to be utterly innocent of the crime with which he was charged. Glancing across at the jury, he saw that they were staring stonily at Dave Travis, probably relishing the thought of seeing him kick out his life at the end of a rope.

'I would like to call David Travis,' announced Jerry, with a confidence that he was anything but feeling deep within.

When Travis entered the witness box, Jerry could not help but admire the sight. It was awful at such a serious time to find oneself distracted by such things, but he had sanded and varnished the wooden surround himself and felt now the satisfaction of a master craftsman in seeing how fine it looked. He managed to drag his mind back to the business in hand and said, 'Mr Travis, would you tell us a little about your life, before coming to Mineral Springs, that is?'

'That's easily done,' said Travis, in his clear, pleasant voice. 'I grew up in Arkansas. My father ran a factory, making farm machinery. I helped him run it up to three months ago.'

'Could you tell us, in your own words, what happened to upset your life?'

From his position on the raised dais, Judge Singer growled, 'Whose words you think he's going to use, if not his own?'

'I was crossed in love,' began Travis, 'My fiancée left me for a man whom she supposed to have better prospects than I.' He stopped for a moment, evidently affected by speaking of this painful matter.

Jerry Freeman said, 'Take your time Mr Travis, I'm sure this is painful for you.'

'He in more pain than Mr Fallon there, as has lost his only child?' asked Judge Singer. 'Don't answer. Let's get on.'

'I left my home, I was that distracted, and took to the roads. I have been moving from place to place ever since.'

'In other words,' asked Jerry. 'You come from a respectable background and are well known as a decent and God-fearing man in your home town?'

Travis shrugged, looking a little abashed. 'Well, I wouldn't have quite put it so myself, but yes, that's about the strength of it.'

'Would you tell us what befell you and Maria Fallon last week?'

'You mean when she was . . . hurt? Sure. I went for a walk with her, up into the hills. Two men came up on horseback and they were crude and offensive about Maria. I conceived it to be my duty to protect her and the result was that I had a fist fight with the two men.'

'What happened then?'

'One of them must have hit me from behind and I suppose that they knocked me about when I was unconscious. When I came round, Maria Fallon was lying next to me. She was dead.'

'Did you harm her?'

'I did not.'

Jerry sneaked a quick look at the jury. It was perfectly obvious that they didn't believe a single word of all this. Some were looking restless and bored, as though they just wanted to get on with finding this wretch guilty and hanging him, a few were glaring at Travis with loathing and detestation in their faces. There was not the remotest chance that he would be able to secure an acquital here and if he didn't take some dramatic action, he would be compelled to watch the brutal death of a man who he was convinced was quite innocent of the charge against him. There was nothing for it, he was going to be obliged to throw in his lot with Dave Travis and take any measures necessary to see that he was freed from the predicament in which he found himself now, through no fault of his own.

Meanwhile, Judge Singer was looking as though he were ready to ask the jury to consider their verdict. He said, 'That all, young man?' to Jerry.

'Not quite, your honour. You said earlier of the defendant, I made a note of your words here. Ah yes. You said,

'We'd need to speak to folk as has knowed him all his life, if we want to know what sort o' man he is.' That is precisely what I believe we should do. Before continuing with this trial, I wish to call character witnesses to attest to Mr Travis's truthfulness and previous good record.'

There was a stunned silence, nobody quite knowing what to make of such a suggestion. At length, the judge said, 'He's from Arkansas you say? How you planning to do that?'

'The same way that you yourself communicate with distant places, your honour,' said Jerry, which caused Judge Singer to furrow his brow and glare angrily at the young attorney. 'By sending message via the railroad and getting wires sent to the sheriff's office in his home town and also his family. We'll soon find out what sort of a man we are dealing with here.'

At first, Judge Singer was inclined to be furious at this new development. He had specially arranged for a reporter to come and cover this trial and it would reflect badly upon him if he now refused a request such as this. Then it occurred to him that this was not really a bad scheme at all. Indeed, it might be the best thing that could have happened. He could now adjourn the case and everybody who wished to see the climax, including the hanging, would need to come back here on a second occasion. It would be like those serialized books that one saw in magazines. They made sure that folk would get that magazine week after week.

'You want that we should adjourn, so's you can make enquiries, that it?' asked Singer.

'Yes, your honour.'

'I can't see why not. See me later an' we'll set down what needs to be done. You're right, we must give the 'cused every chance to prove his case. Two weeks should do. Case will resume in two weeks' time.'

Many of the people who had come to

Mineral Springs just for the hanging were grumbling outside the courtroom. They had been cheated of an entertainment which they believed had been promised to them. It was undeniable though that this adjournment had increased the drama associated with the trial. Listening to the casual conversation in Main Street, it wasn't hard to gather that most of those who had come today would be making every effort to come again in a fortnight.

After Travis had been returned to his cell, Jerry sought an interview with him. To his amazement, the fellow seemed downcast and gloomy. When Jerry entered the cell, Travis said, 'I suppose that you want some details now, so that you can wire my home town.'

'That's right. Then the judge and I will agree what to ask and so on. If we send this off on a train today it should be wired to your town tonight and we'll have the answer back in a few days. Cheer up. At least you still have a good chance.'

'Yes,' said Travis, 'that's true.'

'I'm going to come by again this evening. You might want to get some sleep before then,' said Jerry in a low tone, so that the man outside wouldn't hear. Travis looked up in surprise and was about to ask what Jerry meant by this, until the other held a finger to his lips.

Singer had arranged for there to be somebody sitting around outside Travis's cell practically the whole time. Jerry wondered how he had managed to get these men to give up their time like this, but he supposed that some of them owed the saloon keeper favours of one sort or another. He hoped that there would be one of these men keeping guard that night.

After leaving the courtroom, the attorney headed over to the livery stables on the edge of town. He had noticed that there were horses in a field nearby and that the tack was stored in a barn nearby. Because Mineral Springs was such a little town, with everybody knowing everybody else, he had a suspicion that there would be no night watchman or anything of that sort after dark. He knew that the fellow running the stables didn't live on the premises, which was handy. Standing there, apparently idling his time away, Jerry selected two likely looking animals. Having done this, he went back to The Texas Rose, where Clayton Singer was in an affable and expansive mood. 'Freeman, my boy,' he said, when he spotted Jerry, 'come and have a drink with me.' This was so unexpected that Jerry went over to the judge. 'Not here,' said Singer in a conspiratorial whisper, 'come out back.' Thoroughly mystified, Jerry Freeman followed Singer behind the bar to the pantry.

The noise from the bar-room was deafening, Jerry had never seen the place so crowded and it occurred to him that this might be part of the reason why the owner of The Texas Rose was in such an amiable frame of mind.

'Well, boy,' said Singer. 'You pulled a regular flanker there and no mistake. Could o' knock me down with a feather when you said that about wiring Arkansas. Hooee, that gave me a start. But know what? It's all turned out f'the best after all.'

'Glad that your sales of whiskey are up,' said Jerry.

'Ah, come down from that high horse. You had a good time too.'

'Good time? A man's life is at stake.'

Singer gave him an odd look and then he said, 'Listen, that bastard's goin' to hang, no matter what some sheriff in Arkansas says. I don't care if his pa is the archangel Gabriel and his ma's the mother o' God herself. I'm telling' you now, that fellow killed Maria Fallon. You bought him another two weeks of life, is all. You think my jury's goin' to let him walk free? Don't see it mesel'.'

'You're something else again, you know that?' said Jerry, his temper rising. 'You stand there now and tell me a man's going to hang, just on account of you decide he is a murderer? What are you, God almighty?'

Clayton Singer was in such a good mood, that even this outburst did nothing to dent his spirits. He said, 'No, I don't reckon as I'm God. I say I'm better at spottin' a wrong'un than you. Comes o' havin' been on the earth a good deal longer, that's all. Happen I ain't got your education or brains. I don't need 'em. My job is to rid this area of villains.'

'By hanging innocent men.'

Singer laughed out loud, which infuriated Jerry. After his laughter had turned into a coughing fit, from which it took him a minute or two to recover, Singer said, 'You 'member that Mexican feller as you buffaloed a jury into setting free, first day you fetched up here?'

'Carlos Robles? Yes, I recall him. You nearly had him hanged on the spot.'

'An' you let him walk. Know what he did when he left Mineral Springs? Went straight off and stole a horse, over in the valley along the way. Stole a horse and then teamed up with another man to rob a farm-house. Got killed doin' it, for which we ought to be thankful.'

'There was no real evidence against him . . . '

'No,' said Singer, 'But me and others knew deep down he was guilty an' you came along and upset it all. You was wrong 'bout him, same as you're wrong about Travis. He's a killer an' he's goin' to hang.'

* * *

In his room, later, Jerry Freeman thought over what had been said. It didn't alter his plans at all, but he was at least honest to admit to himself that Singer might have had a point. Although the saloon owner was not articulate enough to put all that he meant into words, the gist of it was that the refined legal system operating in civilized places like New York was no use for a rough and ready place like Mineral Springs. Probably, not a one of those men who had been hanged here over the course of the last decade would have been convicted in a court of law in a big city like Chicago or New York. Like as not, they would not even have progressed beyond the committal stage. At the same time, Singer might very well be right and those men might have been guilty as sin and deserving of hanging. This was a troubling conundrum, but he did not intend to let it change his mind about what he planned to do that very night. Maybe Singer was right and Carlos Robles had been a thief and rustler, but Jerry was as sure as he could be that Dave Travis was not a rapist and murderer.

At about five, the attorney went out to the store to buy some food and a couple of canteens to carry water. Mr Cartwright was serving and he was pleased to see Jerry.

'Good evening, Mr Freeman,' he said. 'How may I help you?' When Jerry had told him what he required, Cartwright said, 'I guess you must be sorrier than anybody, 'cept her pa of course, about Maria.'

'Yes, it was a terrible thing to happen.'

'It's right Christian of you to defend that drifter, even though you must be heartbroken.'

'Heartbroken?' asked Jerry, a little startled.

Mr Cartwright smiled at him. 'Hey, it's all right. Albert Fallon told us how you were sweet on her and how as he hoped that you and she would get together.'

This was the first intimation that Jerry had that people in Mineral Springs thought that there had been some kind of understanding between him and Maria Fallon. He didn't like to disillusion the store keeper and limited himself to saying again, 'Yes, it was a terrible thing.'

After he left Cartwright's store, Jerry wandered down to the livery stable again and was pleased to see that the horses that he had chosen earlier were still in the corral. It also looked as if the place was shut up for the day, but he could see that the barn door was wide open and that the tack-room had not been locked up. So far, everything was going just as he could have hoped.

Looking at the horses that he proposed to steal brought it home to Jerry that what he was proposing was the commission of a capital crime. If he was caught stealing a horse, he was liable to hang for it. The thought made him sick to his stomach, but he was still determined to forge ahead with it. He would never be able to look anybody in the face again for the rest of his life if he didn't take any risks to rescue that man from the death which surely awaited him here.

After speaking to Singer, he was even more sure that this was the correct course of action to take, because he knew for certain-sure that whatever he said and did, that jury was hell-bent on convicting Travis and seeing him hang. Jerry was not in general a man for taking firm and decisive action, but this was a matter of life and death. Not acting now would be like standing on a river bank and watching a man drown without raising a finger to help him. It would be morally reprehensible.

By the time that dusk came, everything was ready. The attorney did not see his way clear to taking his bag with its books in, but then books and clothes could always be replaced; a man's life could not. He carried with him the food and the two canteens full of water. He also had a stout length of wood, wrapped up in one of his shirts, so that it would not look too alarming. Thus equipped, he headed with slow and reluctant steps towards the courtroom where Dave Travis was currently being held.

The door to the court was open, and he could see the glow of a lamp within. The cell was situated in the far corner of the building which had, until recently been a barn. Sitting by the door of the cell was some crony of Clayton Singer's. There was a storm lantern hanging from a nail banged in the wall above him and the man was reading a newspaper.

'Hallo Mr Freeman, didn't expect to see you here this late. That was a right smart stroke you pulled this afternoon. I thought Clayton would have had a seizure!' The man laughed softly, before recollecting himself. Then he added, 'Little enough good it'll do yon fellow in the long run, but least you won him another two weeks of life.'

'Tell me . . . ' said Jerry. His mouth was so dry and his heart was pounding so violently, that he wondered if the man would notice and raise the alarm. But that was crazy, who would suspect a lawyer of being up to no good? 'Can you unlock the door so that I may consult with my client?'

'Sure thing,' said the man and stood up, taking a key from his pocket. He turned round and unlocked the door to

Travis's cell and as he did so, Jerry Freeman swung the piece of wood he was carrying hard against the side of the fellow's head.

9

The man who had been guarding Dave Travis fell to the floor like a poleaxed ox. Without wasting a second, Jerry reached down and unbuckled the gun belt, removing it and then fastening it around his own waist. Travis appeared at the open door of his cell, his face looking grim and pale in the lamplight.

'What's the game?' he asked.

'No game,' said Jerry curtly, still unable to believe what he had just done. 'It's life and death for you. Me too now. They're fixing to hang you, no matter what. Come with me now and we are going to get a couple of horses and then get as far from Mineral Springs as we can.'

'Atta boy,' said Travis admiringly. 'Why, I wouldn't have thought you had it in you.'

'Come on, let's make tracks.'

The two young men walked out of the courtroom and Jerry led the way to the lively stable. He was enormously thankful that there still didn't appear to be any sign of life around the place. He said, 'Can you tack up a horse?'

'You bet I can.'

The two of them went into the barn and took down two saddles and bridles. These, they carried out to the corral and they tacked up the two horses that Jerry had earlier identified as being suitable. When that was done, they rode out of Mineral Springs and headed north.

At first, the two men alternately galloped and trotted their mounts, with the aim of putting as much distance between them and the town as was humanly possible. It was a bright, moonlit night and the track along which they rode was in reasonably good condition. Jerry was terrified of laming his horse and thus being stranded within a few miles of Mineral Springs.

After a space, they began to cut down on the speed a little, cantering and then letting the beast walk for a few minutes. Jerry didn't much want to talk, he was still too much appalled at what he had done. There was also the sharp fear of the consequences of his actions catching up with him. He had an idea that when Clayton Singer found out about his betrayal, to say nothing of the horse theft and assault on a friend of his, the first thing Singer's mind would turn to would be thoughts of revenge. At a guess, that revenge would not entail a trip back to town with all the fuss of a formal trial, but would be more likely to end with he and Travis being hanged on the spot.

'I'm mightily obliged to you,' said Travis, when once they were trotting at a constant speed. 'I thought I was going to hang this afternoon and now look at me, out on the road with a horse between my legs again. I am more grateful than you will ever know.'

'I wouldn't have slept easy,' said Jerry. 'Had I not made every effort to free you.'

'Yes, but stealing horses! Truly, I didn't think you had it in you.'

'It's nothing. Let's talk about something else.'

'I hope we don't bump into some of those ghost dancers I heard tell of.'

'Ghost dancers?' asked Jerry. 'Who are they? You're not scared of spooks?'

'Spooks? Hell, no. I'm talking of Indians. There's some kind of madness sweeping the reservations, with a prophet getting them all stirred up. He's preaching peace and love, but some of those boys are more interested in doing away with the white man than loving their neighbours.'

They rode along in silence for a space after that, both sunk in their own, individual thoughts. Jerry was starting to do what he should have done before this escapade, which was work out how he would get himself safely back to New York. His parents were not rich, but they were sufficiently well-off that they would be able to wire funds to a bank in a city or large town: money that would enable their son to buy a railroad ticket. To that extent, his exile here in Texas had been a bit of a game. At the back of his mind, he had always known that when it came down to it, he could apply to his family for the wherewithal to get him back home. Whatever he had done in Mineral Springs, it was unlikely in the extreme that the consequences would follow him fifteen hundred miles to the east coast. He wondered what Travis would do. Pretty much the same, he supposed.

Jerry Freeman's reverie was broken, when Travis asked, 'What do you think those men back in Mineral Springs will do when they find out the score? Reckon they'll come after us?'

'I shouldn't wonder if that's not exactly what they do,' said Jerry grimly. 'That so-called judge, Clayton Singer, is a vindictive fellow and will take it as a personal affront that I have set you free. Yes, I dare say he will get a posse up and come after us.'

'You think we should stay on this

track or make off across country?'

'I don't take to the notion of riding over rough country at night. I can't see any posse being raised until morning. I say we carry on like this until first light and then, when once we can see the ground a little better, we strike off and head away from the road.'

'You have a genius for crime, you know that? I'm lucky to have secured the services of such an attorney.'

Something was troubling Jerry about the man whose escape he had lately engineered. When he had been in that cell and also in the courtroom, David Travis had been the meekest and most respectable of individuals. It was his general manner when he had been visiting him in his cell which had persuaded Jerry Freeman that here was a man who could not do a beastly or dishonourable thing to save his life. Now that they were out and free, there was an altogether different air about the man; he seemed almost reckless and devil-may-care. Still and all, Jerry didn't know how he himself might react if he had been under expectation of death and then suddenly freed. Perhaps he too would be buoyant and a little exhilarated.

Another difference that Jerry Freeman noticed about the man at his side was that in his cell, he had been an open and confiding sort of fellow, somebody that Jerry could imagine spending a pleasant evening with. Now, Travis was taciturn, hardly seeming to wish to engage in conversation at all. So the night wore on, with increasingly little talk between the two men as dawn approached.

'I think it's time we thought about leaving the road and heading across country,' said the attorney. 'We can see well enough now that the sun has risen. I don't want to be overtaken on the road by Clayton Singer and a band of his friends.'

'That makes two of us,' said Travis, with a laugh. 'I saw enough of that bastard in the courtroom.'

This really came as a shock. If he'd been asked yesterday about this man, he would have taken oath that he was a real gentleman, someone that you would never hear using curse words or being abusive. He looked sidelong at Travis, but there was nothing to be read in the man's face.

'We can't ride all the day through,' said Jerry. 'The horses will need a rest and so shall we.'

'What do you suggest?'

'Maybe keep going until we're a few miles from the road, out of view of it and then rest up and eat. The horses can graze and regain their strength.'

A half hour later, they put this plan into execution and stopped on the far side of a little hill, so that they could not have been seen from the track which they had been following since they left Mineral Springs. The two of them ate some bread and cold meat and washed it down with draughts of cold water. Travis said, 'I've not thanked you properly for freeing me from that place. It was the deuce of a thing for you to do and at risk to your own neck as well.'

'Don't talk about any risks to our necks,' said Jerry, his hand straying unconsciously to his own neck, which he caressed thoughtfully. 'I'd rather put off all such talk until we're sure that we're out of danger. What was that you were telling me about the Indians last night?'

'I only know what I've read in the newspapers. There's some Paiute prophet called Wovoka, away over in Nevada. He's started this thing called the ghost dance religion and it's causing a whole heap of trouble. There's been fighting not far from here. The Kiowa have a different slant on the business from Wovoka and say that God wants them to cleanse the land of the white people.'

'That doesn't sound too promising.'

'No, that's what I thought. We'll have to keep our eyes well and truly open. They say that some of the Kiowa have left the reservations and are wanting to go and join the Sioux for a big war.'

Jerry shook his head sadly. 'Those days are gone. Right or wrong, this is the white man's land now.'

The two of them slept fitfully for two or three hours, both waking up from time to time with a start, convinced that their pursuers were upon them. There were still a few hours to go before noon, when they set off again, heading north east. 'How far to the state line, do you suppose?' asked Jerry.

'Which one?'

'I don't know. Oklahoma must be the nearest, wouldn't you say?'

'I don't rightly know. I don't recall ever having been in this neck of the woods. I guess we just keep riding north and hope for the best.'

The important thing from Jerry's point of view was for them to get out of Texas. He knew enough law to know that once out of the state, it would prove next door but impossible for them to be handed back on any warrant short of murder. The South was still keen enough on states' rights that they would not be about to allow any sort of violation of their own rights and privileges. Once they were in Oklahoma or Arkansas, they would be safe from pursuit. Mind, he couldn't believe that they would really have to get that far, even. How far would Clayton Singer and his boys be prepared to chase them for? The real hazard was not any legal action involving the Sovereign Republic of Texas; it was Singer catching up with them and just stringing them up without a trial.

Travis was still not overly communicative, answering when he was asked a direct question, but otherwise tending to give no more than a grunt of assent. He surely was like a different person since his release. The man himself interrupted this thought, by saying, 'Look back. We have company.'

Jerry looked back and saw that in the distance — he could not gauge how far with any degree of accuracy — dust was being kicked up by a body of riders.

'There's nothing to say that they're looking for us,' he said uneasily. 'At this range you can't even see how many there are, let alone who's among them.'

'You think that if you want,' said Travis, shortly. 'For my part, I'm going to act on the assumption that we have a necktie party on our trail.'

Jerry's heart gave a lurch and he felt suddenly sick with dread. What had become, in retrospect, a bit of a lark had now become a deadly serious business likely to end in his death if things went wrong. He said, 'We'd better go a bit faster.'

Dave Travis flashed him a smile, saying, 'You got that right!' They urged on their horses and in a few seconds were galloping hell for leather across the landscape. Jerry was a competent horseman, having grown up with a pony of his own, but Travis was superb. He and the horse worked as one and Jerry was put in mind of the legendary Greek centaurs. Truly, Travis and his mount seemed like one being. Jerry was constantly having to kick, squeeze his knees together, pull on the reins and make a dozen other movements to keep his horse doing what she was bid. Not so Dave Travis, who just appeared to sit gracefully and at ease upon the animal's back. If he was giving instructions to his mount, then Jerry for one couldn't see him doing it. It was as if the horse and man were linked together by some invisible force, which meant that the animal knew automatically just what Travis required of it.

Of course, they couldn't maintain this pace for hours at a time, but then again, neither could the riders behind them. When they slowed down to a trot for a bit, Jerry said to his companion, 'Where did you learn to ride like that? I never saw the like!'

Travis seemed pleased at the compliment, but he was vague about where he actually *had* learned to ride so skillfully, saying merely, 'Oh, you know. I've been around a bit.'

It was perfectly plain that the riders behind were following them. Really, Jerry had known this all along. Why on earth should a group of riders leave the road and pursue just exactly the same course as he and Travis? Unless, that is, they wanted to catch up with them? As the hours passed, it became increasingly obvious that there was a posse behind them. The distance between them and the men riding after them did not diminish, but neither did it grow any greater.

'I mind that we're going to have to let the horses rest for spell,' said Jerry. 'There's no purpose in riding them to death.'

'Then what?' asked Travis scornfully. 'Sit here and play cards until your friend Singer catches up with us?'

'Not hardly. See over to the left there, that little group of hills?'

'Yeah, what about them?'

'I say we slow down a bit and then head towards them. We're not going to be able to lose those men out here in the open, assuming that they are after us.'

'They're after us all right,' said Travis grimly. 'I know the look of a posse. I'm telling you now, those men are chasing us.'

They changed direction and veered off towards the hills, which, as they approached them, were revealed as being more like a miniature mountain range. It was a curious rock formation, rearing up from the plain. The ground did not slope gently up into these craggy outcrops, but they rather thrust themselves from the grassland, as though erupting fully formed from the earth beneath.

'That's an odd looking place,' said Jerry. 'I hope there's some path or track leads up towards the top.'

Any uncertainty as to whether the riders behind them were really on their tail had vanished since the two men had altered their course. No sooner had Jerry Freeman and Dave Travis turned in their path, than the other men had done likewise. Even more alarmingly, it appeared to Jerry that the gap was closing between them and their pursuers.

By the time that they reached the steep slopes and cliffs of the limestone crags, it was perfectly plain to both men that the posse was gaining on them. Worse, their horses were flagging and if they didn't let them rest soon, there existed a very real possibility that one or other of the animals would simply stop dead.

By good fortune, a crevice in the rocks, which at that point were almost like a cliff face, showed that a manageable, if steep, way led up into the rocky hills. The walls of rock rose on either side of this slope, leaving a winding path which was barely fifteen feet from side to side. It was of slippery limestone, covered in moss and it would have been madness to attempt anything faster than a walk up it. The two men dismounted and led their horses as fast as they could, up into the rocks.

'There's one thing,' said Travis. 'If we can't ride here, then neither can they. All we can hope is that we can find somewhere to hide out.'

'How many of them do you think there are?'

'I'd say seven. Not enough so that they can afford to split up to search for us up here. We're lucky that that was all they could raise to come after us. It could be worse.'

Once again, Jerry was struck by the extraordinary *sang froid* that his companion was displaying. He was himself on the point of becoming hysterical with fear, but Travis was taking the whole thing in his stride, as though they were out in a boat and a storm had come up. He was excited, but not in the least fearful, at least if Jerry judged the matter rightly. Indeed, he almost thought that the man had become more alive since he knew that the posse was on their tail, like a sportsman faced with a stiff, but not daunting, challenge. You're a strange one, thought Jerry

Freeman to himself. I wonder what happened to that diffident and good-natured fellow with the open face and agreeable nature that I saw in the cell? Still, there would be time enough to ponder such questions when once they were free from the threat of lynching by Judge Singer and his men.

Travis said, 'Hold up a second, let's see if we can hear anything.'

They stood there in silence for a while. The only sounds were the strenuous breathing of the horses and the cry of a bird, far overhead. 'Well, they aren't right on top of us yet, at any rate,' said Travis with satisfaction. 'And look here now, here's an encouraging thing.' He pointed ahead.

The canyon along which they had been plodding, alongside their horses, opened out on to a plateau of rock. This was split into a network of gullies and other little crevices and canyons, some of which were big enough for them to enter with their mounts. 'Why,' said Jerry. 'This is a regular maze. If we now dive off into another of those pathways, say that gully over yonder, then we might be able to lose those men entirely.'

'You might be right at that.'

They chose another narrow gully which wound up into some higher slope of the plateau. Apart from the clip-clop of their horses' hoofs on the bare rock, there was dead silence.

'Least the horses are getting a rest,' observed Travis. 'I felt sure that mine was about to drop dead back there.'

'I had much the same feeling,' said Jerry. 'One thing is certain, there'll be no galloping on this rock. It's as slick as you like and covered with green.'

'We're not out of danger yet,' said Travis and no sooner were the words out of his mouth when a figure leapt on him from above.

At this point in the gully through which they were walking, the rocky faces on either side rose to ten or twelve feet above their heads, meaning that they were only able to see right ahead of them. Whoever this was had evidently been stalking them from above, and had now taken the opportunity to attack. For a few seconds, Jerry was so paralysed with surprise, mingled with stark fear, that he was unable to react at all to this event. He just stood there, staring stupidly as the stranger grappled with Travis. Then he recollected himself and drew the gun at his hip. Jerry Freeman had had little experience with firearms, other than shooting out in the woods with a scatter-gun. His main fear was of killing Dave Travis by mistake.

The young attorney raised the pistol and aimed it at the struggling men. He had at first taken it more or less for granted that they had been ambushed by the posse from which they were fleeing. He had assumed that the men from this group had somehow got ahead of them and had now jumped them. By the time he raised his gun to fire, it seemed to Jerry unlikely that this was the case. After all, there was only one man here and neither sight nor sound of anybody else. Surely, the men from Mineral Springs would have stayed up on the rocks and called on them to surrender, rather than leaping recklessly down on them in this way.

All these thoughts flashed through Jerry's mind in a second or two. When he actually focused on the fight taking place in front of him, he saw that this was most definitely not a member of any posse from Mineral Springs. The raggedy figure wrestling with Travis was, for one thing, an Indian. He had no gun and was armed only with a knife, which he was attempting, with great vigour, to stick into his adversary's throat. Travis had a grip on the man's wrist, which prevented the Indian from using his knife, and the two men rolled around on the rocky floor of the gully, each frantically seeking an advantage over the other. Jerry called out, in a thin and reedy voice, 'Hey, just let him alone there!' As soon as he had spoken, he knew that this was sheer foolishness and that the only way of resolving this situation would be for him to kill a man. He took careful aim at the Indian, but neither he nor Travis would remain still for even a second. It was hopeless; he could not possibly fire under such circumstances. Then, his chance came.

Somehow, the Indian succeeded in throwing Travis against the side of the gully, where the other man's head banged on the rock and he lay momentarily stunned. The Indian then bounded to his feet as though he were made of India rubber and gave a cry of exultation. This slight display of bravado proved to be his undoing. As he stood there, about to spring at Travis and cut his throat, Jerry fired once. He thought at first that he had missed, because he had a vague idea that when you shot a man, he kind of flew backwards or something. The Indian, though, just carried on standing there.

Just as Jerry was lining up to take another shot, the Indian began making a strange coughing or hawking noise, like he had something stuck in his throat. Then he gave a convulsive jerk and retched. To Jerry's unutterable horror, a great gout of blood gushed from the man's mouth and he dropped to his knees, still making those peculiar choking noises. Then he keeled over and lay still. Meanwhile, Travis, having recovered from the stunning blow which his head had received, stood up and came over to where Jerry was standing. He said, 'You took your time there.'

Jerry Freeman turned to look at the man with whom he was travelling, the individual for whom he had risked everything; up to and including his own neck. There seemed nothing to say and so he went over to the Indian to see what was what. He found that his bullet had taken the fellow through his throat and that he must have choked to death on his own blood. It was a hideous sight and suddenly, it was all too much for him. He stumbled off and vomited profusely, until there was no more bitter bile left to bring up.

'We'd better not stay here any longer,' called Travis. 'We still have that posse to worry about.'

When Jerry came back to where the horses were waiting patiently, Travis said to him, 'First time you ever saw a man killed, eh? Yes, it's the hell of a thing.'

The words were meaningless. Travis might be saying that it was the hell of a thing, but he was comporting himself as though a bloody death of this nature were just one of those little hitches which were bound to crop up during a journey. Jerry shook his head in disbelief and said, 'What's wrong with you? I just killed a man. He's dead.'

'Yes and if you hadn't killed him, he would likely enough have killed me and then you too. I'm grateful and all that, but we still got to get moving.'

10

After another twenty minutes travelling, the two men came to a point where the gully along which they were walking divided into two. It really was like a maze up here on the limestone plateau. The odds of anybody being able to track them through these paths was exceedingly slender. It wasn't like travelling over grass or through a wood. The bare rock gave no indication at all that anybody, either man or horse, had passed that way. Unless the men in the posse split up and tried to search every canyon, crevice and gully on this rocky massif, there was next to no chance of their being able to pursue the two fugitives.

'What say we take a proper rest?' said Travis. 'I could surely do with one and I dare say the horses could as well.'

Since they appeared, at least for the

time being, to have shaken off the men who were hunting them, Jerry agreed to this proposal. The two of them sat down on a couple of rocks and had another bite to eat. 'You all right now?' asked Travis.

'I'll live. Which is more than can be said about the fellow I shot.'

Travis looked a mite irritated at that, as though he thought that Jerry was making too much of what was essentially a matter of little import. He said nothing though for a space and then remarked, 'He was a Kiowa. I wonder what he was doing up here on his own.'

'On his own? What makes you think that? I shouldn't wonder if his relatives and friends are somewhere nearby.'

'There's a thought. You might be right about that.'

'You think this fellow that went for you was part of this trouble you were telling me of, this ghost dance business?' asked Jerry.

'It's likely enough. The Kiowa and

Comanche are quiet enough these days. It's been a good long while since anybody was attacked round here by Indians. We'd best have an eye out for them as well as that damned bunch from Mineral Springs. Thing is, Indians are apt to make a good deal less noise about their approach than white folk. We'll hear any posse of white men coming from a mile off, but that's not how it's like to be if a band of Kiowa are on our track.'

This was the longest speech that Jerry had heard Travis make since they had teamed up together. He noticed that Dave Travis's conversation concerned itself almost entirely with the here and now and that at no time did he talk about what he had done or would be doing in the future. Still, Jerry hadn't talked a whole lot about this himself. He said, as a way of opening up a little talk on the topic, 'I'm thinking that I shall wire my family for some money, if we get out of this fix in one piece. This sort of life isn't for me at all, I'd be better off back in New York.'

'Yeah?' said Travis, without showing any interest. 'I guess you know best.'

'What about you?' persisted Jerry. 'You think you'll go back to Arkansas?'

'Could be,' said the other indifferently.

'You sound as though you have something on your mind.'

'I'm thinking about that posse.'

'What of it?'

Travis said, 'It's mighty strange that we haven't heard hide nor hair of them since we've been up here in these hills. Our own horses are making the devil of a racket on these stony ways. Not only that, there's seven or eight men. You'd think they'd be talking, making some noise. Just listen now.'

The two of them listened. There was nothing at all, except in the distance, the occasional bird calling.

'What's more,' continued Travis, 'you might have thought that shot would create some interest. I don't think that they followed us up here at all.'

'You think they turned back?'

'That'd be nice, wouldn't it?' said Travis, smiling. 'No, I don't think that for a moment. They followed us this far and were closing on us. No, I think they're still around.'

'Well then,' said Jerry, slightly nettled at the know-it-all attitude of the other man. 'What do you say is happening?'

'I think they're still down there on the plain. How big do you suppose this stony outcrop is? It puts me in mind of the bluffs you get in some parts, where a mass of rock just sticks up from level ground.'

'You mean,' said Jerry thoughtfully, 'when we've finished roaming around up here and head back down to the plain, they'll be waiting for us?'

'Yes, that's what I mean.'

'What should we do?'

'I think, head on as we were and hope that we miss them. They might figure we'll double back. Or again, they might be waiting just exactly due north of us, in the direction we were going. We can't calculate how they'll play it. One thing is for sure, we can't stay up here for long. There's no chance of any food and I think you're right, that Kiowa probably has friends in the area. Sooner we get back down to the grasslands, the healthier, I reckon.'

They carried on leading the horses north, using the sun, which was an hour or two past its zenith, to orient themselves. Jerry was no woodsman, but he knew well enough that at noon, the sun is just precisely due south in the sky. So walking away from it between, say ten and two of the clock, will take you roughly north.

Travis showed no inclination to talk more as they moved across the limestone plateau and that was fine with Jerry Freeman, because he had some hard thinking to do and the less chatter, the better. He had somehow had a picture in his mind, back in Mineral Springs, that when he had sprung Travis from that cell, that he,

Jerry, would lead them to safety. But the boot was all on the other foot now and he couldn't for the life of him figure out how that had come to pass. After all, what would the well-to-do son of a factory owner know about adventures of this sort?

They came to a pool of fresh water, a natural cistern where the rainwater could collect. Jerry filled up their canteens, which were all but empty and then they allowed the horses to drink their fill, being careful not to let them foul the water as they did so. Travis looked at the two animals critically and said, 'That's one more reason why we have to start making our way down to the plains.'

'What's that?'

'Those critters need food. We need to let them graze for an hour or two. They could do with some oats really, but I can't see that happening.'

'You fond of horses?'

'Wouldn't say that I'm exactly fond of them, no. They're useful for getting you from here to there.'

'It's odd that you turned up at Albert Fallon's farm on foot. I'd have thought that you might have left home on a horse.'

Travis turned to face Jerry. His eyes were completely cold and his face an expressionless mask, as he said, 'Anybody ever tell you that you ask a lot of questions?' He kept his face absolutely blank and wholly devoid of any human emotion and to Jerry there was something terrifying about this, almost as though he were looking at an animal that has somehow managed to assume human form. Then Travis turned away and the spell was broken. The episode left an unpleasant taste in Jerry Freeman's mouth though.

As Travis had guessed, the plateau on which they were wandering was not a vast one, being no more than eight or ten miles across. If it had not been for the fact that they were compelled to weave back and forth along the gullies and crevices, they could have walked from one side to the other in three or four hours. When first they began exploring the place, they had been aware that there was always a gentle slope upwards, in the direction in which they were travelling. For the last few hours though, they had been moving gradually lower. Rather than the plateau being quite level, it was in fact a very shallow dome.

The two men did not exchange another word after leaving the water-hole. For his part, Jerry had been unnerved by that blank and expressionless face which Travis had turned to him. What the other man was thinking of, the attorney neither knew nor cared. His chief aim now was to get down from this place and find his way to a town. The sooner he and Travis parted company, the better that Jerry would like it. He had always prided himself upon being a sound judge of character, but he had surely taken a wrong turn here. This was a very different man indeed from the one who he had visited and consoled in his cell.

Towards late afternoon, the little canyon in which they were moving suddenly and unexpectedly opened out, and they found themselves standing on a spur of rock. From this vantage point, they could not see the plain surrounding the bluff, but could see quite some way into the distance. On the horizon was what looked to Jerry to be a substantial town. He had no idea if this place would prove to be in Texas or Oklahoma, but he decided then and there that it was where he was heading, once they found their way down from here.

'Any idea what that place is?' asked Travis.

'None in the world. Could still be Texas, maybe Oklahoma.'

'Don't know about you, but the sooner I'm out of Texas, the better I'll like it.'

Jerry said, 'Yes, I feel the same way.'

Still leading their horses, they made their way along a broader path than before. This one didn't have rocks towering on either side. It was very noticeable now that they were descending; the slope was becoming increasingly steep. The further they went, the more the plain between them and the distant town gradually came into sight.

'Not far now until we reach the grass and we can ride again,' said Jerry. 'I'm getting a little tired of this walking game.'

Ahead of them was a line of rocks, with no apparent way through them. These were huge boulders, some of them the size of small houses. They turned to the left and began seeking a way through this seemingly impenetrable barrier. Eventually, they came to a gap between two boulders and Jerry said, 'Thank the Lord for that.' He started forward and then drew back in dismay. They were now only about fifty feet above the grassy plain which surrounded the rocky hills in which they had been wandering for a good part of the day. A gentle slope led down to the open country and the town for which they were heading could only be five or six miles away at most. It wasn't the town that Jerry was looking at though and which had caused him to shrink back in fear. Not a hundred yards away, Judge Singer and a half dozen men on horseback were waiting for them. Travis had been quite right, the posse had simply ridden as fast as they could around the bluff and banked on them carrying on north and descending at this very point.

'What is it?' said Travis angrily, as Jerry backed up his horse into him. 'What are you playing at?'

'Singer and his boys are waiting down there.'

'Ah shit, I knew it. Did they see you?'

'No, I don't think so.'

'Let me think for a minute,' said Travis. After a bit he said, 'I've got the germ of a plan. Say we lay an ambush for them here and then lure them on.'

'What d'you mean, an ambush?'

'We could let ourselves be seen, but

not before we roll some of them smaller boulders there and bring them to this gap. Then when they start up the slope towards us, we roll down the rocks. You got ammunition in that belt as well. We'll be firing from cover and they'd be coming up that bare rise. I reckon we could kill every mother's son of them before they reached us.'

Jerry was horrified at this suggestion. He said, 'You mean kill all those men without giving them a chance to defend themselves? No, it's not to be thought of.'

'Well then give me the gun. It's my skin at stake too. If you're yellow, I don't mind doing it all myself.'

'No, I won't hear of it.'

The two men faced each other and Travis looked as though he was about to hurl himself forward and take the weapon that Jerry was carrying by main force. They stood like that for a second, as though posing for a tableau in a waxworks, but then Travis said, 'What's that? Is that them coming on?' He darted to the gap through which they had earlier intended to pass. Carefully, so that the men below would not catch sight of him, he peeped round the rocks. Then he gave a satisfied laugh. 'I reckon you and me have been getting ourselves all riled up for nothing. Our problems are all solved.'

'What can you mean?' asked Jerry.

'Come see for your own self,' said Travis. 'Only mind nobody catches sight of you.'

Jerry Freeman went up to where Travis was standing and peered cautiously round the rock. The posse were in the process of moving off, but it did not look as though they would make it. Two parties of Indians were converging on them at the gallop. There were a few shots and then the Indian riders crashed into Singer and his men. For a while, there was a confused mêlée and it was impossible to make out what was happening. In a short time, the fighting was over and every one of the white men either lay dead on the ground or were slumped lifeless in their saddles. Some of the Indians dismounted and removed the dead riders from their horses, throwing them down carelessly, like they were sacks of potatoes. A couple of warriors went round, slashing open the stomachs of the corpses. It was all too much for Jerry, who retreated back behind the rocks. Travis though was entranced, looking to Jerry like a man who is attending a particularly enthralling theatrical show.

The thought of all those men being massacred put Jerry in mind of the man he had himself killed only a few hours earlier. The thought made him feel ill again and once again, he found himself throwing up. Travis looked round upon hearing his retching and said mockingly, 'You surely do have a sensitive stomach. I don't think that you're cut out for this kind of enterprise at all.'

Jerry sat down, exhausted and weak. His one and only wish now was to get back to civilization. He supposed that there was a good chance that the

Indians who had lately murdered Judge Singer and the others would make their way up here and finish off him and Travis, but he was just too tired to do anything about it right now.

He must have been sitting there for a good quarter hour before Travis came over and asked casually, 'How are you feeling now. Better?'

'Thank you, I'll live.'

'You'll be glad to hear that our redskin friends have ridden off, taking all the horses with them. I thought for a time that they were going to come up this way, which would have meant death for us, but they went skittering off round the edge of this thing. I'm thinking that the way is open for us to cut along out of it. We'll give those Indians a little time to leave and then we can be on our way.'

'Were they more Kiowa?'

'I guess. They have a big grudge against us from a few years back, when they were all driven out of Palo Duro and so on. They surely have messed up those men that were riding after us. Ah, they say it's an ill wind as blows nobody any good. They did us a favour, anyways.'

'Is that all you can say?' said Jerry. 'Seven men are butchered in front of your eyes and it doesn't make you sick or even bother you?'

'Hey, those boys were aiming to put a rope round your neck as well, you know. The Indians did you a favour too. What's to worry about?'

Something else had been nagging away at the back of Jerry Freeman's mind during the day and it was at that moment he realized what it was. When first he had met David Travis, the man had represented himself as the son of a wealthy factory owner. He had been well spoken, courteous and quiet; as befitted that role. Now, Travis was not only more aggressive and coldblooded, but his very voice and accent had changed. It was nothing that you could properly place your finger on, but the man was somehow more vulgar and coarse than he had been in Mineral Springs. He was using cruder words and slurring his words a little. Jerry found himself nursing the horrible suspicion that Travis had been playing an act before and that only now was he seeing the real man; the man behind the mask.

'Well?' said Travis.

'I'm sorry, what did you ask me?'

'I asked what you had to worry about?'

'From the posse? Nothing, I suppose. You're quite right.'

'You are a worrier, you know that? I spotted it when first you came to see me after that little misunderstanding back in Mineral Springs. Soon as you walked in that cell, I said to myself, Lee, that man is one of God's worriers. Always fretting over what has happened and things that may never happen. I was right, wasn't I? For God's sake, lighten up, man.'

'That's enough of the profanity,' said Jerry sharply. 'I don't care for it.' Then something hit him most powerfully. He said, 'Lee? I thought your name was David?'

Travis shrugged. 'Lee's my middle name.'

Their eyes met and in that moment, Jerry Freeman had a flash of terrifying insight and knew that he had made the worst mistake that he had ever made in the whole course of his life. He had been so keen on being the man in the right and the one fighting for justice and a host of other things which made him feel big and important, that he had blinded himself to the simple and ghastly truth. Something of this must have shown in his face, because Travis said, 'You all right there? You look like you're going to throw up again.'

Jerry shook his head, not trusting himself to speak. Travis was right, he did feel sick again, but it wasn't a physical sickness; he wasn't about to start retching. It was a hundred times worse than that. He said, 'I'm fine. Let's get moving again.'

Travis was watching him warily. He said, 'I sure hope we understand each other.'

'I think we understand each other just fine.'

The other man nodded and they led their horses through the gap in the rocks and down to the plain. In a hundred yards or so, they came across the bodies of the erstwhile posse. Every one of them had had his stomach slashed open after death. 'They do that as a favour to them,' explained Travis. 'It lets out the spirit of the fellow, so's he can fly off and join his ancestors.'

11

Jerry Freeman wandered among the corpses, wondering what on earth he had done. He was as sure as he had ever been of anything in the whole course of his life that these men's deaths lay at his door. Had he not undertaken his rescue mission, all seven of these people would have been at home with their loved ones in Mineral Springs. It was the hell of thought. Travis said, 'There won't be anything left. The Kiowa will have looted those men of anything worth shit.' Once again, Jerry was struck most forcibly by the vulgarity of the man he had freed. Not only his tacit assumption that the only reason that he himself would have for looking at these dead men would be to see if there was something worth stealing, but also by the awful, crude language that he used to express himself.

'I didn't have it in mind to steal from the dead, no matter what they might have on them,' he told Travis. 'I think I should say a prayer.'

'Just as you will, but the day's wearing on. We don't want to be here if those Indians return.'

Jerry turned away in disgust and looked down at the faces of those men who were laying on their backs. The first he saw was Clayton Singer. The man looked older in death than he had in life. Maybe it was because he had always seemed so irritable and vigorous, but the attorney had pegged him for a man in his late forties. Looking now at his face, it was clear that he was closer to sixty. Near to Singer was the owner of the livery stable, who presumably had a more personal reason for riding after the fugitives than merely that of seeking justice. He had lost two horses and a couple of saddles.

Looking at those seven dead men, it

seemed to Jerry that he was vouchsafed some kind of revelation. These deaths were the price of his vanity, his need to act as though he knew better than others. He had looked down on those small-town hicks, because he was a New York attorney who had attended the best law school in the country. But that wasn't really worth a damn, because an old scoundrel like Singer had been better able to spot a wicked man than him, for all his lack of anything but a rudimentary education. Jerry said softly, 'I'm sorry, your honour. I would have done better to take heed of what you said.'

Travis said roughly, 'You finished fooling around with those bodies yet. I want to reach that town before dusk.'

'Yes,' said Jerry. 'I've finished now.'

'Thank Christ for that,' muttered the other irreverently.

Down here on the grasslands, the town looked a good deal further off than it had from the vantage point of the rocky hills. The horses were sluggish and tired, stopping often to graze. Neither Jerry nor Travis hurried them along, because the creatures obviously needed to eat. They had not been properly fed for the better part of twenty four hours now, most likely.

The sun was sinking low over the horizon to their left, turning a dull red as it did so. Travis had not spoken since they had left the remains of the posse and he looked to Jerry to be sunk in a blue study. Maybe it was the setting sun, because that sometimes makes folks feel a little sad. So they plodded on, both men wrapped up in his own thoughts. Jerry was the first to break the silence, by saying, 'Will you go back to your father in Arkansas? You know, the factory?'

Travis laughed. He said, 'You know, don't you?' He turned round to look at Jerry and his eyes widened in shock when he found that the young lawyer had drawn his pistol and was pointing it straight at him.

'What is it I know, Travis? That

you're a liar and a play actor? Yes, I reckon I have figured that out well enough. That you played me like a fish on a line and copied how I spoke so that I would feel more sorry for you? I know that too.'

'Took you long enough to work out though, didn't it?' said Travis, apparently not in the least degree discomposed at looking down the barrel of a forty five. 'I wondered if I was laying it on too thick when you came to visit me in that damned barn, but I couldn't have been. No sir, you swallowed the whole thing, hook, line and sinker.'

'Yes, it was a good act, I'll grant you that.'

'Come on man, you didn't like that judge any better than I did. Don't start shedding tears over him now. It's true what I said to you back there on the trail, that posse would have hanged you, same as they would me.'

'Maybe I deserved to hang for springing you.'

'Ah, that's a lot of foolishness.

There's no harm done. Come on, put up you gun and let's be on our way. I'm still worried that those Kiowa will come by and catch us out here in the open.'

'Are you?'

'Yes, I am. And I tell you now, I don't take to having guns pointed at me. I owe you a lot, but don't go getting me vexed now.'

'Why, what would you do about it? You don't have a gun, do you?'

Travis bit his lip and looked hard at Jerry, trying to fathom out how much danger he was in. Now that he had a fair idea of what sort of man this was, the lawyer could pretty well work out what was going through Travis's mind. In the first instance, he was wondering if he was in imminent danger of being shot. Then again, he was probably considering the chances of Jerry handing him over to the law in the town to which they were heading.

'So what are you going to do,' said Travis. 'Shoot me? I don't think so.'

'I want to know the truth, that's all.'

'What the hell for? You're not a priest or something of that sort. What do you care about the truth?'

'In the last twenty four hours, I have committed theft, broken a man out of custody, shot a man dead and now I'm responsible for the death of seven other human beings. You don't think I have a right to know what it was all for?'

Travis was still watching him narrowly and Jerry guessed that the fellow was trying to work out whether or not he would do better just to turn round and gallop off or perhaps even to attack him and deprive him of the gun. For the time being, Travis evidently decided that the safest and wisest course of action was just to wait quietly and see what would develop.

'All right then,' said Travis. 'Out with it. What would you know?'

'Who are you? I mean really. I am not a perfect fool, I can see full well that you aren't the son of a prosperous factory owner.'

A peal of hearty laughter greeted this

statement. ‘Factory owner? Lord, I wonder I could have kept a straight face with that one. If you’re asking about my father, then I can tell you now that I never had one, or leastways, not one I ever met or heard tell of. Go on, what’s next?’

‘How do you live?’

‘What is this,’ asked Travis, a flicker of amusement in his eyes. ‘An interview for a post with a bank or something? I live how I live, moving from place to place as I please.’

‘Doing what?’

‘Whatever I damned well please. Come on, let’s end this nonsense and get back on the trail. I don’t want to be out here after dark. You saw for yourself how matters stand with the Kiowa. I’m telling you straight, this is going to end with us having our throats cut.’

‘Doing what?’ asked Jerry again.

‘Stealing, robbing, working sometimes. Any damn thing to make ends meet. There now, is that enough for you?’

'You ever been tracked by a posse before today?'

'Yes. Can we get moving now?'

'Not yet. Why were you being pursued before?'

Jerry knew why he was asking all these questions. He had an unpleasant duty to perform and he was hoping to delay it for as long as was humanly possible. More than that, he was trying to make some sense of this whole business and thought it fair to allow Travis the opportunity of explaining and perhaps even justifying himself.

'Listen man, you're not a priest nor yet a doctor. Why would you care about all this? I was being chased before on account of I had stolen some fellow's life savings. He was an old boy and there had been a bit of a scuffle.'

'Was he hurt?'

'No, he was killed.'

'You killed him?'

'Not exactly. He was grabbing at me, there was a tussle and he went over. Banged his head on the fireplace and I guess his skull was weaker than most. I was hardly to blame.'

Looking into the man's eyes, Jerry could see that he really and truly believed this. He was an innocent man, trapped by an unfortunate circumstance and then chased for something he hadn't done. That, at any rate, was certainly how David Travis believed matters to stand. Maybe, Jerry thought, he had not met enough bad men in his life to judge these things, but there seemed to him to be something lacking in Travis. This was not a bad man trying to defend himself; it was a man who didn't even know that he was bad.

'That the only death you've been connected with?'

'Pretty much, I suppose.'

'Pretty much? What the devil does that mean?'

'I mean until just recently.'

At these words, Jerry Freeman felt as though he had received a blow to his stomach. He had been hoping and praying that he was wrong and that despite the way all the evidence was stacking up, he was mistaken in his suspicions. Hearing it confirmed from the man's mouth still came as a shock. He said, his voice barely audible, 'You mean Maria Fallon?'

'Sure,' said Travis, shrugging casually. 'Who else did you think?'

'So you do mean her?'

'Well then,' said Travis. 'Yes, I meant Maria. She was one sweet girl.'

'What happened?' asked Jerry Freeman, his voice barely above a whisper.

'Yes, I don't wonder you would ask such a question. She talked about you, you know? Said she didn't think that you noticed her as a woman. I think she might have thought that you were on the other side of the tracks, if you know what I mean. One of those who doesn't go a whole heap on women.'

'You better leave that alone, Travis.'

'Hell, I'm only saying. I could tell what she wanted. She saw me watching her, you know. Flaunted herself, like. Women like that, knowing that a man is watching them in that way.'

'Do they like being beaten round the head with a rock, as well?'

'Ah, that wasn't rightly my fault.'

'No, I thought that it wouldn't have been. What chanced?'

'What do you think? I went for her, she played hard to get, like it was game of kiss-chase in the schoolyard. I surely didn't mean for her to die.'

'Strikes me,' said Jerry, 'that you are a most unlucky man, with people falling dead around you like that.'

Travis shrugged impatiently. 'All right, you've had your say. I told you about it all. What now?'

'One last thing. How did you get so banged up yourself?'

'Oh, that. That was nothing. I just banged a rock about a bit on my forehead and so on. You'd be surprised how much blood you can get to flow that way.'

'Didn't it hurt?'

'Are you kidding? It hurt like hell. It was that or hanging though and I figured being hanged would hurt a sight worse. Now, is *that* it?'

Jerry Freeman shook his head sadly. He said, 'I guess you couldn't believe your luck when a fool like me came along.'

'Come on man, we have to go. I'm leaving, anyway.' Travis started his horse moving and the lawyer called out to him: 'You stay right where you are, Travis.'

The other wheeled his horse round and said, 'That girl was right about you, you know. You're not a real man. I'm not afeared of you in the slightest.'

'Damn you!' said Jerry Freeman and shot him dead.

12

As Jerry approached the town, he thought about what had happened and decided that he had at least put one thing right. Travis had been like a mad dog. He looked human on the outside, but within, he was no more than a beast. Judge Singer had seen it well enough and knew what he was dealing with. The old man had a deal more wisdom in some ways than Jerry did, or maybe it was just that he was older.

It would not have been right to let a man like Travis loose again, because as sure as God made little apples, there was a man who would rob, rape and kill again, as soon as the opportunity presented itself to him. Shooting such a man was a duty to the world. It disturbed Jerry Freeman that he had behaved the way that Singer would have done, but there it was. Maybe sometimes, lynch law was a necessary adjunct to the civilized administration of justice.

The closer he got to the town, the bigger it looked. There were telegraph poles running alongside the railroad that ran into the town, which mean that Jerry would be able to wire his parents in New York. He supposed that he should wire Emma as well and let her know that he was safe and well. He didn't rightly know what his plans would be once he got home, but they probably wouldn't involve working for some big commercial concern. There was a lot that needed to be done in the country, many things wrong that had to be dealt with. Making himself a pile of money was perhaps not at the very top of Jerry Freeman's list of priorities, the way that it had been when he had bought that railroad ticket south. He would need to talk to Emma about it and see if the two of them couldn't come up with another plan. It surely would be good to get home and see her again.

We do hope that you have enjoyed reading this large print book.

Did you know that all of our titles are available for purchase?

We publish a wide range of high quality large print books including:
Romances, Mysteries, Classics
General Fiction
Non Fiction and Westerns

Special interest titles available in large print are:
The Little Oxford Dictionary
Music Book, Song Book
Hymn Book, Service Book

Also available from us courtesy of Oxford University Press:
Young Readers' Dictionary
(large print edition)
Young Readers' Thesaurus
(large print edition)

For further information or a free brochure, please contact us at:
Ulverscroft Large Print Books Ltd.,
The Green, Bradgate Road, Anstey,
Leicester, LE7 7FU, England.
Tel: (00 44) **0116 236 4325**
Fax: (00 44) **0116 234 0205**